Miranda Writes, Honor & Deceit

Frank Santorsola & Christina Santorsola

Greg & Kel

Best Wishes,

Uncle Frankie

&

BAXTER

Aunt

Chrissy

Baxter Productions Inc.

308 Main St
New Rochelle NY 10801
www.baxterproductionsmedia.com

ISBN: 978-0-9982773-2-5

Also, by Frank Santorsola

Miranda Writes, Honor & Justice

The Garbage Murders

Preface

The following story, Miranda Writes, Honor & Deceit is a fictional
story. It's the third in a series of three books, *Miranda Writes, Honor &
Justice* and *The Garbage Murders*. Honor & Deceit is the account of
Frank Miranda, an undercover detective assigned to the Westchester
County District Attorney's Office, who is targeted for death by a
terrorist who is also planning kill as many infidels in New York City as
Allah wills. The story chronicles Frank's relentless attempt to find out
why he's marked for death and stop the senseless killing of innocent
men, women and children by this radical Islamic terrorist.

The book is written by Frank and Christina Santorsola. It's our hope
that the reader will travel with us through the many nuances of this
story as we ignite the reader's imagination and take them along during
Frank's relentless efforts in apprehending international terrorists.

To all the men and women in law enforcement who sacrifice so much,
we say bravo. Men and women in blue truly make our society a safer
place to live so that we the people of the United States can enjoy the
inherent freedoms of life, liberty and the pursuit of happiness.

Chapter One

"Hurry or we'll miss our flight home," I said in a rushed voice, "there isn't another one off this island till tomorrow!"

"We'll be on time, don't worry," Denise replied.

How did I ever get here in the first place? I asked myself. Denise was the answer. Denise and I have been dating for a few years. Her best friend Sofie, married into rock 'n' roll royalty. Sofie Koprowski was now Sofie Plimpton wife of Terrence Plimpton and mother to his three sons, seven-year-old Terry, five-year-old Denny, Denise's godson /namesake and two-year-old Elton. Yes, his godfather is Sir Elton. Sofie has achieved great success since being crowned America's Next Top Model eight years ago. The rest is history, a fabulous history.

Terrence Plimpton is the lead singer-songwriter of the wildly successful "Touch of Terrence" rock group phenom. Sofie and Terrence asked us to join them for a week at their fully staffed luxury home in Bora Bora. It was a week of rubbing elbows with some of the other mega stars who vacation there. It was an eye opener seeing how the beautiful people live and love. When it's all boiled down, most of them are rather down to earth people, just like us, with a few obvious exceptions. In any case we were treated royally. Several of the guests were fascinated with my police undercover work. They couldn't get enough of my stories, and believe me; I've got plenty of them. One of the guests was Thibaut Laura. Thibaut is 6 feet 4 inches tall, charismatic and the consummate bon vivant. He rose from meager beginnings in a small village near Cannes, Tourette du Chateau in the South of France. Now he is CEO of the Onorine Group, a worldwide chain of five-star hotels. He currently lives at his flagship hotel, Onorine Un here on Bora Bora.

Now we're heading back to reality - JFK via LAX. After seven days of Mahi Mahi, Foie Gras, Papaya Puree and the national dish of the island, Poisson Cru, I'll be back at my usual New York City haunts dining on burgers and brews. Somehow being with Denise makes it all seem perfect either in French Indonesia or in New York, NY.

It's been a year since Denise and I moved into a fifth floor walk up in Bronxville, NY. We rent a roomy one-bedroom apartment that has Denise's artistic touches throughout. We first met at Jake's Bar & Grill in New York. This drop-dead gorgeous girl was sitting alone at the bar. Of course, I pulled up a stool next to her. She looked like a Sports Illustrated cover model, 5'8", sharp facial features, sultry green eyes, and blonde shoulder length hair that bounced around her neck when she laughed. She was easy on the eyes and much easier to talk to. The outfit she was wearing was just as provocative as she was. She was dressed in a low-cut pink cashmere sweater, blue jeans and knee-high leather boots. In a short time, it felt like we had known each other for years. Denise said that she'd been approached by a few modeling agencies but wasn't interested in pursuing a modeling career. Geology is her field of choice. She loves the outdoors and loves to spend her time off hiking and rock climbing.

First day back on the job, I tried to re-orient myself with my usual routine. I usually get to my desk early to be sure I'm on top of my game. If I have time, I work out at the gym three days a week and I meditate fifteen minutes a day. These disciplines, along with an occasional game of golf, help to keep my mind, body and spirit in balance. My work schedule is erratic and I need the regiment to keep me on steady ground. After tying up some loose ends on that first Monday back, I got a message that one of my former informants, Mike Baraka, wanted to meet me ASAP at his apartment. I could always count on Mike for valuable information, he rarely let me down. Together we've worked on some of the most successful drug cases the DA's office has ever seen.

I got into my candy apple red Corvette. It was seized by my office during a drug raid last year. Unfortunately for Milton Camps, drug dealer, I'll be enjoying this sweet ride while he relaxes in prison. I headed to Maple Street to see Mike.

Chapter Two

I woke up with a throbbing headache, my heart and head were pounding. I tried to pry my eyelids open but it hurt too much. I must have been sleeping like a bear. I don't remember falling asleep. I don't remember much of anything right now. Did I drink myself into oblivion last night? I started to feel very anxious, I sensed something was wrong. "Detective Santorsola, are you awake?" a gentle voice said. "Frank, can you hear me?"

I heard but I couldn't respond.

"Squeeze my hand if you can," the voice continued.

I weakly squeezed a hand, it was the best I could do. I didn't have any other ability to communicate. "That's good detective, squeeze as hard as you can." I gave another faint but successful squeeze. I could sense some fumbling around with my bed and heard what sounded like a beeping monitor. I opened my eyes at half mast to a big blur. Several shadowy images were quickly moving around me. "Detective Santorsola, can you hear me? This is Dr. Fishbach." I mumbled a guttural reply. "You suffered some trauma but you're gonna be okay. Can you nod your head if you understand me?" I moved my head slightly down toward my chest. "Good detective, now get some more rest."

Bright sunlight awakened me. I forced my eyes open and tried to look around at my surroundings. Where the hell was I, a hospital? I saw a call bell looped around my bed rail, I rang it furiously. Two nurses came running in. "It's good to see you alert detective. We've been watching you very closely," said one of them.

"Where am I, why am I here?" I groaned. I tried to push myself up in bed. The nurses quickly guided me back down. "Try to relax; you've been in a medically induced coma."

"Just stay put, Dr. Fishbach will be here soon. She will explain everything to you," said one of the nurses.

"Can I have some water?" I asked.

"Right away," said the younger nurse.

Doctor Susan Fishbach entered the room. I could see a little more clearly now. She was tall, blonde, long legged, in her mid forties, and wearing the usual medical garb. "Detective Santorsola," Dr. Fishbach said in a monotone voice, "ten days ago you were injured when a bomb exploded. The impact of the explosion caused you several injuries, but most heavily affected your upper body. You have a major concussion and several broken ribs. We have kept you sedated so that you could heal."

"Explosion?" I asked. "What the hell do you mean a bomb went off? Where?"

"Captain Matthews will be here shortly," Dr. Fishbach replied. "He will fill you in. In the meantime, you will need to rest, and continue to get your strength back."

"My vision is blurry," I said in a low panicked voice, "will that improve?"

"Yes," she replied, "it is to be expected after such trauma. You should regain full, clear vision soon."
I nodded slowly and said, "Thank you doctor."

Captain Matthews arrived a few minutes later. "Frank, how are you feeling?"

"Like I threw myself on a live grenade," I replied. "What happened to me?"

"Well," he said, "you're damn lucky to be alive. All we know is that you were on Maple Street, as you entered Mike Baraka's building, there was a huge explosion. It was a bomb. It blew the entrance apart and you with it. You were catapulted out into the street. Do you remember anything about it?"

"Nothing," I replied, "I can't remember a fucking thing. The last thing I remember is driving in the Corvette, heading somewhere."

Matthews, a strapping Irishman, in his fifties, graying at the temples, stood over me and said, "Frankie, we've got a lot of investigating to do. Do you think you were the intended target of the bomb?"

I shook my head and replied, "I don't know."

"I know you've got plenty of enemies out there." Matthews continued.

Just then Nurse Shanequa interrupted us. "Gentlemen, my patient needs his rest. I'm gonna let his girlfriend and his brother in here for a few minutes, and that's it for the day."

"Okay," Matthews replied, "Frankie, I'll be back soon."
A few minutes later, Denise and my brother were by my bedside. Denise leaned down and gave me a gentle kiss on the lips. "Are you okay?" she whispered.

"I think so," I replied.

Our lips were nearly touching. "I've been here everyday, waiting for you to regain consciousness," Denise said softly. "I thought I was gonna lose you." Tears streamed down her beautiful face.

"I knew you'd make it back to us," Richie said, placing his hand on my hand. "I know how strong you are." I'm a few years older than Richie and we are extremely close. It's hard to tell us apart even as we've gotten older. If it wasn't for my mustache, most people would think we were twins. Rich and I are in our thirties and both are 5 feet 11 inches tall and have a full head of dark wavy hair.

I must have dozed off again. My next recollection was DA John Xavier Hogan paying me a visit. I was barely able to discern his robust stature. "Frankie, everyone in the office is so relieved that you pulled through this ordeal," Hogan said. "The doctor tells me you should be able to go home in a few days. Rest is imperative, so you take as much time to recuperate as you need. We're all pulling for you Santorsola."

"I'll be getting a daily update on your condition, hang in there."

"Thanks, Mr. Hogan," I groggily replied.

As Hogan left, my mother walked in. It was time to face the music. "Filio mio," my mom said in her native Italian. She stroked my forehead, "What have they done to you?"

"C'mon ma," I whispered. "They haven't done anything to me. I'm okay." Holding my hand, my mom continued to rail on in Italian, worried about me. She also worries that Helen, my ex-wife, would keep the girls from her if anything happened to me.

"Helen would never keep the girls from seeing you ma," I said.

My mother hit me right where it hurts the most. My daughters Catie and Francesca were so young. Catie was only four and Francesca was eight years old.

"Franco, the job is…a…too…dangerous. You…a…need…a…to…quit."

"Ma," I said, "I'm a cop. This is what I want to do with my life, you know that."

My beautiful mother Inez nodded and squeezed my hand tightly. This spit fire of a woman knew that I'd never quit police work. At age sixty-eight she keeps many of the old world customs. She dresses in black, out of respect for my father Frank who passed away a few years ago. My mom has a fiery temper and is quick to erupt. She takes no guff from anyone. Richie and I both know that she's the glue that holds our family together. She complains that there isn't enough time in the day for her, between working at the local Italian American grocery store, and caring for my 87-year-old grandfather, Guarino, who doesn't need to be cared for. My grandfather moved into my mom's house soon after my dad passed away. He now spends much of his time at the Italian American Club arguing with his friends about today's politics and playing Briscola, a traditional Italian card game.

As my mom was about to leave she stroked my cheek and said sadly, "Franco, please let nothing happen to you."

 Forty-eight hours later I was evaluated and approved for release from St. Johns Hospital in Yonkers, New York. Denise arrived in room 103 to gather me and my belongings for the victorious ride home. My brother Rich and Joe Nulligan, my partner, helped us remove all the flowers, and baskets that so many well wishers had sent to me. An orderly came in with a wheelchair. "Not for me!" I barked. He replied, "It's hospital policy, sir. Sorry."

I reluctantly accepted the ride. As I was wheeled out of the hospital, I was greeted by hundreds of police officers and hospital staff cheering me on. It was a touching tribute and a deeply moving experience that I will never forget.

Chapter Three

Denise and I arrived home and settled in. I dominated the living room and made it my perch in the daytime. My vision was back to normal but I was still in a great deal of pain, so I continued to take the prescription pain killers.

Chief Christopher insisted on posting a security detail in front of my apartment to prevent anymore mishaps. Naturally, it was a great relief to Denise, she was anxious about the situation.

A few days before I was to return to work, Mike Baraka paid me a visit. "Come on in Mike."

"Hey Frankie," he said with a smile, "how you feeling? I was told that no visitors were welcome till you regained most of your strength. I was worried sick about you," Mike explained. "I kept in touch with Joe Nulligan, he asked me not to contact you till today."

"Yeah Mike, everyone's concerned about me recovering and keeping a very low profile. The truth is, I really needed the rest and relaxation. It helped me bounce back to almost 100%."

"That's terrific," Mike replied.

"I'm returning to work in a few days," I remarked.

"That's great news buddy," Mike responded. "I was questioned by your office about the message you were given to meet me the day of the explosion."

"Message from you?" I asked. "I don't remember any message from you Mike, I'm drawing a blank."

"Maybe that's when you were driving to my house!" Mike exclaimed. "Nulligan told me you were responding to a message that I left with Detective Carol Szeeba for you that day. Detective Szeeba told Joe that she got a call from me, but it was an imposter. Somebody lured you to my building and tried to blow you up."

"Fuck, Mike," my voice raised. "I gotta find out who did this to me and why. I'm gonna need your help."

"You know I'd do anything for you," he replied, "anything."

The next morning, as I was about to leave the apartment, I felt a dull pain in my head and popped a pain pill. I lost my balance and fell onto Denise's dressing table. I hit it so hard that I almost knocked the mirror attached to the table off its hinges. I pushed myself up from the hardwood floor; I fell again, lost my balance and ended up back on the floor. My ribs were aching. I reached for my forehead to see if I was bleeding from the stitched wounds. Thankfully, I wasn't bleeding and I was still in one piece. I slowly picked myself up and hobbled over to the bed-side chair.

A few days later, I was ready to go back to work. I was free from pain pills; it felt wonderful to be useful again. It isn't easy for a guy like me to be pampered and waited on. Getting back in the swing of things was going to be the best medicine for me. DA Hogan conducted a meeting early on my first day back in the squad. The usual suspects were in attendance, ADA Beau Winslow, Chief Larry Christopher, Captain C.J. Matthews, Angel Serrano and of course, my partner, Joe Nulligan.

Chief Christopher greeted me with a huge grin when I walked in. Larry Christopher is one of the youngest Chief of Detectives the Westchester County District Attorneys Office has had. He's forty-five and good looking. This blue eyed blond carries his six foot athletic frame well. It's rumored that his wife has a problem with alcohol. At last year's Christmas party, his wife Alice had one too many drinks. She babbled without making sense to some of the party goers. The chief was clearly embarrassed. He guided his wife out of the party by her arm. They didn't look like the happy couple everyone thought they were.

"Good morning," DA Hogan said, "first things first, welcome back Frank."

"Thanks Mr. Hogan," I said with a slight grin. "I'm glad to be back."

"Gentlemen," Hogan said, "this office is making every effort to solve the Maple Street bombing. No stone will go unturned till the perpetrator is brought to justice! What we now know is that squad Detective Carol Szeeba took a telephone message allegedly from Mike Baraka and left it on Frank's desk. Detective Szeeba alerted Frank to the note as soon as he walked into the squad room. The message was for Frank to meet Mr. Baraka at his apartment ASAP. Baraka denies ever leaving such a message for Frank."

We all sat there listening intently to Hogan going over the details of the case. "Frank, have you regained any memory from that day?" Hogan asked.

"Not a shred," I replied disappointedly.

Chief Larry Christopher interjected, "We know that there are a few prime suspects who might want Frank's head on a silver platter, Ayman Hani for one and of course Nick Galgano. I'm sure there are others hiding in the shadows," Larry said. "This was an assault on all police officers. We will solve this."

For the next ten minutes we tossed around a few more ideas about the best way to proceed in the investigation and then Hogan adjourned the meeting.

Back at my desk, my mind wandered to several prime suspects in my attempted demise. Top of my list was Ayman Hani, Mike Baraka's "twin cousin." Years ago Mike Baraka was falsely arrested, indicted and convicted of trafficking heroin from the Middle East to New York for crimes his cousin Ayman Hani committed. After his conviction Mike signed a cooperation agreement with the Unites States Attorney's Office, Southern District of New York, to mitigate his and his sister Delia's ten-year sentences. Under that agreement, Baraka would develop prosecutable narcotic cases in return for his freedom.

Since my office worked jointly on the prosecution of the heroin trafficking case with the US Attorney's Office, I was assigned to work undercover with Baraka to make narcotic cases. When I first met Mike in the United States Attorney's Office, I thought he was of Italian descent. He's tall, dark, has jet black hair and eye-catching facial features. At twenty-seven, this Jordanian American is eye candy for the ladies.

At first it was rough developing a mutual trust, but eventually we worked together like ham and eggs. We were able to bring some big time wise guys and Columbian drug lords to justice. Make no mistake about it; I get a rush from beating these lowlifes at their own corrupt game.

Mike always emphatically declared he was totally innocent of all charges brought against him. Mike steadfastly maintained that his cousin Ayman Hani was the one involved with the drug traffickers and not him. Mike and his cousin looked so much alike that Mike was arrested, instead of his cousin, during the execution of arrest warrants. When I saw that he had the courage of his convictions, I tried to help him right the wrong that had been done to him.

Mike's cowardly cousin high-tailed it to the Middle East as soon as he could, following the arrests of Mike and several members of his family.

They were all found guilty at trial. Ayman Hani's freedom permitted him to lavishly feast on baba ghanoush, falafel, grape leaves and wine while those convicted ate hot dogs and Fritos washed down by 2% milk in an abysmal prison cafeteria.

After Ayman Hani returned from the Middle East, he confessed to me and in doing so cleared Mike of any involvement in trafficking heroin. There are only a small percentage of criminal convictions that are overturned in the United States, Mike Baraka's case happens to be one of them, thanks to my efforts.

I'm sure that Hani has a vendetta against me, as does his partner in crime Nick Galgano. Galgano is a member of a Mafia family who operated in the greater New York area. Nick is number two on the ever growing list of scumbags who would be happier if I disappeared off the face of planet earth. Nick Galgano was also arrested and found guilty of trafficking in heroin. He was sentenced to twenty-five years to life in federal prison. I was responsible for his incarceration and I'm sure he wants a pound of my flesh. Oh yeah, there's one more twist in this ongoing saga. Galgano's only child, Cindy Galgano and Mike Baraka have a newborn son together, Santino. Much to Nick's dismay, Cindy and Mike live together as parents to baby Santino. Nick despises Mike for many reasons, not the least of which is that Mike's an Arab and not Italian, as Nick would prefer. Nick has softened a bit since the birth of his grandson Santino, but not too much. Nick is behind bars for a very long time and is no longer involved in Cindy's daily comings and goings, leaving her free to do as she pleases without constant scrutiny from her father. So much for day dreaming, I need to get back to work.

Chapter Four

Freddy Spina was the mob guy who schooled me and introduced me to the Mafia life. I had my eye on him and one night when the moon and stars were aligned, I sat next to him at one of his usual hangouts, LaFamiglia Bar & Grill in Hell's Kitchen, in Manhattan. We shot the shit for a few hours. Freddy was an associate in Nick Galgano's mob crew. Like mobster Henry Hill, only one of Freddy's parents was Italian. Freddy's mother was Norwegian and therefore Freddy could never become a made man. Both parents must be Italian to be a Uomo D'onore.

Freddy looked like the kind of guy who ran a brothel in another life. Double breasted suits, a pinky ring, a black shirt, white tie and greased back hair completed the picture of this pint size wannabe. Freddy enjoyed the bravado of being associated with mob life, it made him feel connected to something bigger than himself, as is the case for most mob members, I assume. Freddy, AKA, "Far Away" got his nickname because he likes to sing, and when Freddy sang, whoever was listening to his off-key voice asked him to sing far, far away.

Spina played into my well dealt hand. Sooner, rather than later, he introduced me to Nick Galgano and his crew, vouching for my legitimacy. I was now in and had to prove my worth to the Galgano faction. Everybody has a nick-name. Galgano gave me a colorful nick-name *Cheech from Orchard Beach*. Cheech is 'Frank' in Italian; Orchard Beach is a popular Bronx beach. It's a neighborhood thing; imposing aliases has captivated the public since the days of Al "Scarface" Capone. I started running numbers in the back of a fruit stand on 153rd Street and Third Avenue in the Bronx. I progressed rapidly to bigger and more trusted tasks like running my own sports betting room. Freddy always had my back; he got a piece of every dime I made.

Freddy taught me a thing or two. He taught me the fine art of detecting a tail. Freddy drove an old yellow Lincoln convertible. His car was parked in front of the social club in Yonkers, N.Y. As I was about to walk into the club, he asked me to take a ride with him. Freddy said, "Cheech, the first thing you do is to use your side view mirrors as soon as you pull into traffic."

"Cheech," Freddy said, "you want to see what cars pull out behind you. Make a mental picture of them. If one or two cars pulled out, drive around the block a few times to see if they're still behind you. If they are, it's a sure bet that you're being followed."

"Like I say," Freddy continued, "there may be more than one car following you. It's up to you to ditch the tail. Ya don't wanna take em anywhere important. Remember, the first thing before leaving the apartment in the morning is to think cop. It's their business to lock us up. They have their job to do and we have ours."

Freddy taught me how to cook a few delicious Italian dishes like Veal Osso Bucco, Mozzarella En Carozza and Spedini a la Romana. Even though the tiny kitchen in his apartment was cramped, he produced fabulous meals out of the space. The man could cook but only while listening to Sinatra's greatest hits blaring through the airwaves. Freddy was an authentic goodfella. Too bad for him his mother was from Norway.

As I got myself deeper and deeper into Nick's crew, Nick took an unexpected liking to me, an undercover cop's dream. Nick asked my opinion on how to dress, what cologne to wear, what type of car to buy and I gladly obliged. This was the sole purpose of my job, to get as close as I could to the boss without having my true identity revealed. I was bringing in a lot of money for Nick every week and receiving 30% of the action I brought in. Before long I was outshining most of the veterans in his crew. Every illegal dime I made was turned over to my office.

I needed to up the ante and begin to appear to live the part. My office provided me with money to rent a swanky furnished apartment on the Upper East Side of Manhattan. I wore Armani suits and Valentino shirts to cement my persona. I entertained my new-found mafia friends in style, all the more to heighten the game. Freddy and I cooked up a storm. I wined and dined them first class while building a solid case against them all.

I think Nick started to view me as the son he never had, or the brother he lost. I bore a striking resemblance to his late beloved brother, Armando. Everyone commented on our likeness, which must have struck a chord with Nick. Armando was shot and killed during the famous KLM Airway diamond heist at JFK Airport. The thieves got away with the loot, worth many millions of dollars, but Armando was killed in the cross-fire by security guards. Nick kept his brother's framed picture close at hand over the bar in the social club. Nick often gazed up at it, lamenting the loss of his brother.

March 15th, fittingly the *Ides of March*, most of Nick Galgano and his crew took over Ray's Restaurant in East Harlem, New York City. It was Nick's birthday and of course Galgano was able to attain the unattainable, four tables at the star-studded restaurant. Ray's was the hottest ticket in town. Nick treated his top bananas to an evening of authentic old style Italian food and wine in this iconic New York eatery. All the big players were there dining on Nick's dime. Freddy played the piano while Nick serenaded the crowd with Italian favorites. After he had more than enough to drink, Nick sang *Volare and Mala Femina*. Nick had the audience in the palm of his Sicilian hand. He built up to a crescendo for his finale and belted out a heartfelt version of everyone's Italian favorite *Mamma*. There wasn't a dry eye in the house. Nick closed the evening to thunderous applause from every patron of Ray's. The loud applause muted the raucous sound of the FBI and Hogan's office, in conjunction with NYPD, bursting into Ray's arresting everyone at the four tables, including Frank Miranda, who built the case leading to their arrests and convictions. Nick, Michael Calise, Freddy Spina and the rest of the crew faced big time in Federal prison. Nick was really crooning for his *Mamma* now.

The paddy wagons hauled all the stunned, angry men away. A few shit their Versace drawers while others remained calm. It turned out to be one of the largest and most successful busts of its kind with a 95% rate of conviction. Freddy Spina turned state's evidence and worked an immunity deal for himself. It ultimately became known, through discovery proceedings initiated by Nick's attorney, that I was the undercover cop who had provided the probable cause for wiretaps and bugs that took down the Galgano crew.

Freddy entered the witness protection program and was given a new identity. He was relocated to Alaska by a team of US Marshals. He found work as a salmon fisherman for a large fishery on Alaska's Kenai Peninsula. Freddy made friends with one of his co-workers, Jed. It was a welcome relief for the very lonely Freddy. Unfortunately, one day after an exhausting day of fishing, Jed discovered Freddy's cold, lifeless body in a storage container. Spina was shot to death and thrown on top of hundreds of pounds of salmon on ice.

Freddy Spina put a new spin on the old mafia adage, *He sleeps with the fishes*. The mafia's tentacles know no boundaries.

Chapter Five

Back in the day, my best friend Ace and I were inseparable. As early as the 4th grade we bonded for life. We were in the same class throughout most of grade school. Our idyllic days were spent playing stickball in the street, riding our bikes all over New York City and sharing our love of boyhood and all the greatness this city could offer two young chums.

Our families grew close as well and oftentimes would take turns babysitting one of us. Ace and I had everything in common; we were both daredevils, fearless and inquisitive. One of our favorite places to play was Central Park, our 843 acre playground. We felt even more invincible and free when we roamed the "prairies" of Central Park. We could pretend to be anything we wanted, cowboys, firemen, you name it but by far "cops and robbers" was our all time favorite. The only problem being, we both wanted to be the cop and be the one to capture the bad guy robbers. Somehow we worked it out over the years taking turns with some of the other neighborhood kids.

One afternoon Ace and I were passing through Central Park's Strawberry Fields, a 2.5-acre zone created in memory of the late Beatle John Lennon. It's near 72nd Street across from the famous Dakota apartment building where Lennon lived and died. We were approached by three street thugs. They demanded our bikes and threatened to kill us if we didn't hand them over. They were slightly older, bigger and we were out numbered. Ace and I stood our ground as they started their assault. Adrenaline was running through our bodies and miraculously we managed to defeat our three attackers who bore bloody noses and fat lips. Not two boys to act foolishly, we took the first opportunity we could and peddled away like bats out of hell. We were never to come face to face with the bad guys again. We knew we had each others back then and forever. We never shared the story with anyone back then. I suppose we were afraid our parents would ground us, in fear of reprisal from the hoodlums.

Today my buddy Ace and I are still fast friends. I think I'm the only one who still calls him by his boyhood nickname. He's better known today as first grade Detective Sal "Ace" Lifrieri, NYPD, heading up the Intelligence Division currently investigating the Russian Mob. In adulthood, we continue to share good times and bad, fostering our friendship even further.

Ace asked if I could meet him at his command on Hudson Street in New York City. Some new intelligence was available that he thought I would find enlightening. Joe and I took a ride down to Hudson Street, about forty five minutes away in the heart of lower Manhattan.

"Hey Ace, how you doing?" I said with a smile.

He invited us into his office. A huge board with postings and photos dominated the room. Ace explained that Mustafa Salib, a Syrian, made his way into our country. He's an Islamic terrorist, who is notorious for masterminding, planning and executing a number of attacks in Syria and Egypt. He reveled in blowing up Coptic Christian churches in Egypt.

"How do you know all this shit?" I asked.

"We have developed a reliable, well placed informant inside a very active cell in Brighton Beach, Brooklyn," Ace said. "The movement wants the informant to martyr himself so he can have his way with those seventy virgins. He wants to live; he doesn't want to blow himself into tiny pieces just to get laid seventy times. Can you blame him?" Ace chuckled.
"Can't say that I do," said Nulligan with a smirk.

"We refer to the C.I. as Icarus," Ace said. "Icarus exposed another murderous player in this game of *Clue.* Bachelorette # 1, Anna Zharkov, who made her way into Salib's heart by proving herself to be indispensible in obeying his every command."

Ace continued, "Zharkov and Salib both ascribe to the Takfir Ideology, a controversial concept in the Islamic discourse. It's a belief in a form of excommunication or death of any Muslim who is declared impure. The two are feared as the most ruthless of terrorists in New York. They not only are set on destroying us, but as Takfir demands, if they declare any of their Muslim brothers to be heretics, the men are slated for death. For example," Ace went on, "Intel has it that Salib declared Abd Al Bari, a former informant of ours, guilty of Zina, unlawful sexual relations. Zharkov and Salib are judge, jury and executioner under their twisted vision of Takfir. They cut Abd's throat, attached an explosive device to him. They tossed his body into a dumpster and remotely detonated the bomb. They managed to kill three innocent sanitation workers, as well as their traitor. They don't consider themselves to be impure because they are cleansing the world of infidels."

Joe taking it all in replied, "Sal, it sounds like you have some great sources of intel. This is real inside information and gives our side great incite into these *malandrinos.*"

Ace, grimaced and said, "It's a very twisted mindset they have. It's clearly a way for them to masquerade as holy, while killing whoever they please, without any uprisings from the rank and file."

Salib is a master of subterfuge and Anna Zharkov is his willing puppet. As a child she lived in war-torn Grozny, the capital city of the Chechen Republic. The apartment building she lived in with her mother Bozena and five siblings was bombed by Russian forces. She was the only surviving family member. Apparently scarred for life, she ultimately took up arms, turned to a world of violence and revenge. Now, Anna and her associates operate out of Brighton Beach, Brooklyn.

Joe was impressed with the information and said, "Sal, thanks for the information. Please keep us in the loop, great stuff!"

"Gentlemen," Ace continued, "let's go grab an early dinner in Brighton Beach. Wadda ya say? You never know what we might see."

"Yeah, let's go," I replied.

Brighton Beach is all of 3.4 square miles and the home to a bastion of the Russian Mob, Bratva, as it's called. Due to a large influx of Ukrainians into this section decades ago, it's nicknamed "Little Odessa." Everyone speaks Russian. Ace heard that Café Liudmilla had a great reputation for authentic fare. It's clean and casual. We feasted on pirozhok, little pies with a pocket of deep-fried dough filled with meat and potatoes, dishes of pierogi ruskie and blintzes. Dessert was smetannik, a honey cake with sour cream frosting. I plan on going back.

Ace and his group, along with the 60th precinct, have their hands full. In Brighton Beach, last year the crime statistics reflected high numbers of murders, rapes, drug busts, robberies and felony assaults among other crimes. It's said that Italian organized crime in America is a pimple on a horse's ass compared with the Russian mob in America and globally.

We dropped Ace back on Hudson Street. On the drive back to our home base, we rehashed the intel Ace provided and were reassured that there were some vital eyes and ears inside the bowels of the terror cell.

Chapter Six

The Dancing Crane Café in Central Park was a favorite dining spot for many visitors to New York City. Mike Baraka insisted that we meet there for lunch. He said that it couldn't wait, it was urgent.

Mike looked stressed at lunch and couldn't stop fidgeting.

"What's up Mike?" I asked. "Spill the beans, you look a mess."

Mike, dressed like he was going to a fancy restaurant, anxiously blurted out, "Two FBI agents paid me a visit last week."

"What do they want with you?" I asked.

"Frankie, they want me to work for them," he replied.

"How?" I asked.

Mike hesitated for a moment and said, "They want me to keep tabs on my cousin Ayman when he's released from prison next month. Agent Spencer said that my cousin has been radicalized in prison by a blind Muslim Sheik from Jordan. The FBI has information that Ayman has converted to Islam and has been schooled in the Koran over the last four years."

Mike loosened his collar, cleared his throat and continued. "The Sheik is a hard and fast follower of the radical fundamentalist belief that all infidels that refuse to convert to Islam must be killed, children are no exception. Agent Desaye said they would give me a week to think about it. Thank God Cindy wasn't home. She'd freak out."

"Frankie what should I do?" Mike whispered frantically.

"Mike don't do a damn thing," I said. "They can't force you to work for them. Lemme know when they contact you again."

"Okay," he muttered, "I feel a lot better just talking to you." He reached for my hand and shook it. As he was leaving I had a flash back. We were driving over the Brooklyn Bridge to meet a heroin dealer in Brooklyn Heights. At the time Mike was protesting his innocence, saying that it was his cousin Ayman who distributed heroin for Nick Galgano, not him. As we drove over the bridge, I remember him looking at the Statue of Liberty and asking me if I ever visited her. I told him, "Yes, on my third-grade field trip. It's hollow with a lot of narrow stairs that we climbed to get to the top." I remember the somber expression on his face when he turned to me and said, "Frank, I thought it was much more than that. I thought it represented freedom." Later that evening, Mike and I were ambushed during a heroin deal gone bad. Mike took a bullet and fell to the ground seriously wounded. The drug dealers sped away. I ripped off Mike's white shirt and stuffed it into the gaping wound to stop his loss of blood until help arrived. Luckily, Mike made a complete recovery.

Chapter Seven

Enter Detective Sergeant Tyra Williams, a young dynamic cop out of Las Vegas P.D.'s Counterterrorism Unit. Tyra was on lend-lease basis with my office. She was relocating to New York and she was a perfect fit in the DA's Squad.

Tyra and I worked together last year in Vegas and she impressed me with her work ethic and *chutzpa*. We worked together on an organized crime money laundering investigation with tentacles extending from New York to Vegas. We developed a strong attraction for one another in just a few short days. At the time, Denise and I were having a rough patch in our relationship. It was hard for Denise to handle living with an undercover cop and all the trimmings that went with it. Denise eventually walked out on me. During that hiatus, I didn't know if I would ever see her again.

While I was in Vegas, Tyra was involved in a shooting at a fast food restaurant on the strip. She was walking out of the restroom at Pepino's and heard what she thought were firecrackers exploding outside. The doors flew open and a crazed mad-man rushed in shooting an automatic pistol spraying the place with bullets. Thinking fast, Tyra took cover and entered the kitchen area. She drew her weapon and displayed her badge, crouching down behind an overturned table looking for the best vantage point to take aim at 30-year-old Titus Clems, a home grown terrorist and a disgruntled former Pepino employee who was yelling "Allah Akbar," repeatedly on the top of his lungs. Tyra crawled over trembling bodies on the kitchen floor until she got into a good position to fire at Titus Clems. She raised her weapon and shot out the transom window above the entry door. When Titus turned around in response to the blasted-out window, she had his head in her crosshairs. One beautiful well-trained shot to his fucked-up head was all it took. Another one bites the dust. Tyra was a brave cop. She saved many lives that day, one of whom was Mrs. Titus Clems, the manager of

Pepino's who was six months pregnant with a baby girl. It's all in a day's work.

Since we last worked together, Tyra had been promoted to Detective Sergeant. Before starting work in the New York detective squad, she will be attending a conference given by NYPD that will focus on the previous terrorist attacks and their similarities. The modus operandi used in the bombings at Boston, Chelsea in Manhattan and Seaside, New Jersey will be carefully scrutinized. I know she'll want to hear about the incident that nearly snuffed out my life if she hasn't already.

Matthews asked if I'd pick her up at the airport. She'll be staying at the Grand Hyatt on 42nd Street for a two-day conference until her short-term rental apartment is available.

At exactly 4:15 p.m. Tyra walked out of gate 8, pulling a carry-on Louis Vuitton suitcase behind her. She's statuesque and was dressed in a sexy tight fitting white business suit with a knee length pencil skirt and leopard print four-inch heels. What a sight! Her dark eyes, bronze skin and high cheek-bones were the makings of a Vogue model. I was fixated on her deep-set eyes and arched eyebrows which really give her an exotic look. Tyra is half Egyptian and part Moroccan and Welsh. When she saw me, she ran up to me, threw her arms around my neck and gave me a big hug. Damn, those old feelings were stirring. It was like a jolt of electricity sparking through the lower half of my body. Our eyes locked. "Frank, it's been a long time. You look wonderful!"

Shit, I hoped that she didn't hear my heart thumping. "So do you," I said with a gleam in my eye. "It's great to see you. I'll fill you in while we drive to the hotel." I gently put my hands on her waist and slowly stepped back. I grabbed her suitcase and walked out of the terminal to the parking lot. Our conversation flowed naturally. We were comfortable together, maybe too comfortable.

As Tyra and I entered Manhattan, her eyes lit up. "What an extraordinary city! Every time I visit, I fall deeper and deeper in love with it, Frankie. Look at the Chrysler building, a 1930's masterpiece of Art Deco!"

I pulled up curbside at the Hyatt. Tyra, unfastened the seat belt, angling her body, as she inched closer to me. She instinctively placed her hand on my knee, softly massaging it with her fingers. Man, the girl was making me hard.

"Frank, I think about you a lot."

All I could do was shake my head in dismay. I'm not usually shy, but I blushed. I was truly at a loss for words. What could I really say? Look, I'm a man and when someone as stunning as Tyra, throws herself at you, it's hard to resist. She raised her eyebrows, with a questioning look, asked quietly, "Are you still in a relationship with Denise?"

I nodded yes and said, "Yes, I am." As she got out of the Vette, she bent over, leaning down into the passenger side open window, exposing part of her buxom cleavage and said with a come-hither look, "Do you want to grab a bite to eat?"
Those dark sultry eyes were mesmerizing. This woman could make any man lose his sensibility. "Sure," I said with broad grin thinking, and I'm being totally honest here, I needed all the strength I could muster to keep from jumping her bones. "They've got a great restaurant in the Hyatt." She smiled and said, "I'll check in and meet you in the bar." I popped the trunk, got out of the car, ran around to the rear and removed her suitcase. I watched as she rolled her suitcase through the revolving doors of the hotel into the crowded lobby. I parked in a nearby garage.

I made my way through the ornate lobby decorated with expensive artwork, gilded lighting fixtures and Queen Ann style furniture. I asked a bell boy where the bar was, he pointed to a sign, directing me. The bar was jammed. I didn't see Tyra. She was already seated in the restaurant. The sun was about to set and our view of 42nd Street was lit up like a Christmas tree.

A smartly dressed waiter, in a starched uniform, came over to take our drink order. Tyra ordered a Vodka Martini and I ordered a glass of Pinot Noir. We lingered over our cocktails while getting reacquainted. It wasn't until our second round of drinks arrived that we ordered food. We both ordered steaks and truffle fries. We kept the conversation light as we ate. I imagine we both wanted to stay away from talking about what was really on our minds, sex.

She leaned into me, with a beckoning gaze, her full lips parted and said, "It looks like we're going to be working closely together for awhile."

It was now or never. I guess it was up to me to put a stop to this thing before it took on a life of its own. I reached over for her hand, gently taking hold of it, looked dead in her eyes and said as convincingly as I could, "I'm very much in love with Denise. You and I need to keep our relationship on a professional level if we're going to continue to work together. I'm sorry Tyra, I think you're a very beautiful woman, but it's not in the cards for us."

She yanked her hand back quickly, forcing a smile. "I guess congratulations are in order." She was blunt. She said that she still had feelings for me, I just stared back at her. I hesitated to say anything, dropped my head and continued to eat my food. I knew she was upset but she'd have to deal with it. I later found out that she's had a bad relationship with one guy on the job. I didn't plan to be another statistic. I knew I'd better leave before things got stickier.

Denise called. "Frankie, I'm at the 20th Precinct. I was leaving work and a man jumped out of a car and tried to force me into his car."

I blurted out, "Are you okay? Did you see who he was?"

"No, he had on a ski mask," she wept, "I'm safe now. The police brought me here. I need you to come and get me."
"I'll be right there. I'm nearby. Give me thirty minutes."
I explained to Tyra why I had to leave. I sobered up very quickly.

I arrived at the 20th Precinct and located Denise in the office of Captain Mary Reynolds. Denise, trembling, grabbed me, sobbing like a baby. "He tried to drag me into the car," she cried. "I was screaming for help. I tried to fight him off, but he was too strong. Luckily, the security guard saw what was happening and ran over. He fought the creep off and dragged me back into the building to safety."

"Thank God you're okay," I said as I held her tight.

Denise, shaking like a leaf said, "The guy jumped back into the car and the car sped off, but my co-worker got the plate number and called 911."

Captain Reynolds saw that Denise was too distraught to continue and interrupted.

"A white Jeep with those plate numbers was spotted on West 72nd Street. The officers attempted to pull the car over. They turned on the dome lights. The driver sped up. A chase ensued. The Jeep sideswiped a few cars and swerved into a fire hydrant near the Beacon Theater. Two men, Syrian Nationals, here on a student visa, identified as Uday Sader and Yousef Seigh, jumped out of the vehicle loaded for bear. A quick firefight followed. Using their car for cover, the perps fired recklessly, wounding two innocent civilians. They grabbed an elderly woman and used her as a human shield. Luckily one of the responding officers, Officer Cody Chang is an accomplished marksman. He killed both subjects leaving the hostage unharmed. Needless to say, Officer Chang saved untold lives today."

I thanked Captain Reynolds for helping Denise. I called Officer Chang to thank him personally. I immediately requested that two detectives from the squad were assigned to protect Denise. I placed my arm around Denise and said, "Honey, it's okay. I'm gonna take you home now. Nothing like this will ever happen to you again. I promise."

Chapter Eight

I wanted to grab a cup of coffee so I let the office know to radio my security detail. I jumped into the Vette and headed for the Nino's coffee shop. Strong, black coffee always revved me up. I set up my laptop and began to write a complete report, recapping the events that led up to the attempt on my life. Captain Matthews called, "Frankie, we're trying to get to the bottom of that message you got. Someone wanted you at Mike's apartment to take you out. Detective Szeeba is the one who spoke to the individual who identified himself as Baraka. The call was traced back to a burner phone but we were unable to gain any information from it. Now we're back to square one." I replied "That sucks, sounds like a total dead end." "Yes it is but that won't stop us from solving the mystery. Meet me later in the office to explore more options."

About two hours later, I stood outside the shop and casually gazed up and down the street to see who and what's around me. A late model grey Chevy definitely caught my eye. I couldn't see inside; the windows were tinted. I faintly heard the engine start. The Chevy slowly pulled into traffic, heading my way. Something inside me said Frank, something's wrong. You need to protect yourself. I grabbed my pistol from my waist, holding it downward towards the sidewalk. I slowly began to backpedal towards the building. My eyes never left the car as slowed down while approaching me. I waited to see what was going to happen next. I waited for the passenger side window to lower, for the car doors to open, but nothing happened. I'm sure that whoever was in the car saw me begin to raise my weapon. I was ready for the scumbags; I guess they were beginning to have second thoughts about finishing the job. I gripped the gun tighter; ready to send a clip of nine-millimeter bullets, into the passenger compartment. Fuck 'em. It's them or me. The car idled for a moment and then pulled away. I tried to get the plate number, but the car was too far down the block to get the tag number. I waited for a few minutes, studying the street before wiping the sweat off my forehead. I thought to myself, okay, another hand played.

Today there were no winners or losers. One way or another, this situation wasn't gonna end well. My money was on me.

Chapter Nine

"Frankie, pack your bags, we're going to France," Ace said excitedly.

"France? Ace, what the hell are you talking about?" I replied in amazement.

"My bosses had lunch with your bosses and decided we're going!" Ace said. Our C.I. code name, Icarus, in the Brighton Beach cell has credible information of an imminent attack on the Cote d'Azur in the South of France. The C.I. says that Mustafa Salib is somehow involved in the planning of the attack. Our two agencies have arranged for us to travel to France and coordinate our intelligence with the French National Police."

"Okay Ace," I responded, "I have a buddy over there. I'll contact him and tell him we're coming. He's in the hotel business and can make hotel arrangements for us."

"That's perfect Frank," Ace replied.

Ace and I flew Air France to Nice. We were greeted at the (NCE) Nice Cote d'Azur Airport by my Bora Bora buddy, hotelier Thibaut Laura. Thibaut generously insisted that we stay at his hotel in Cannes, Onorine Deux. He made us an offer we couldn't refuse, a complimentary stay that our made budget directors very happy.

I introduced Thibaut to Ace and said, "It's really good to see you Thibaut," as we heartily shook hands.

"Je suis super contente de vous voir aussi," Thibaut replied. He was really glad to see me. "Let's get you settled at my Onorine Deux," he said.

"Looking forward to it," Ace said.

It hadn't been too long since The Cannes Film Festival had wrapped up but there were remnants of it all over Cannes and Nice. Celebrity sightings abound. I'm surprised that an attack hadn't taken place during the festival considering how many people were in town.

The Cote d' Azur is truly one of the most stunningly beautiful sights I've ever seen, another playground for the rich, famous and infamous. Thibaut's hotel in Cannes overlooks Cannes Harbour in the heart of this glamorous city. More than 800 berths are housing yachts and more yachts. Fresh flower markets, shops and upscale restaurants line the streets providing countless hours of entertainment for anyone lucky enough to be there. Tourists gawk at all the topless women on the beaches of the French Riviera. The locals don't stare, it's routine for many women to go topless on the beach.

"What time shall we meet for dinner tonight?" Thibaut inquired.

"I'm afraid, Ace and I have to meet with inspectors from the National Police," I replied.

"I understand," Thibaut replied. "I must insist, the day after tomorrow is a partial holiday for you two. It's Bastille Day. I've made arrangements for us to go to Nice and dine with some wonderful people I want you to meet," he said.

"Sounds like you won't take no for an answer. It will depend on how things develop on our end. So, if it all goes well, we will be delighted to join you."

"Keep in mind you never know how crazy it can get in our line of work," Ace said.

That afternoon Ace and I reported to the office of Inspector Yves Roux. We all buckled down to the business of pooling our resources to thwart any upcoming terror attack on the Gold Coast of France. Many of the inspectors we worked with had a great command of the English language. Mustafa Salib was a name they recognized at once. He was very elusive, yet still managed to rear his monstrous head. Inspector Roux believed our informant's intelligence is on target. Since the Cannes Film Festival and Bastille Day, hundreds of Gendarmerie Nationale Military police have been deployed to protect the citizenry from a possible attack.

At noon, on Bastille Day, Ace and I were able to break free and meet Thibaut at the Olivia restaurant in Nice, eighteen miles north of Cannes. Thibaut introduced us to his brother Jacques, a local accountant and his wife, Thibaut's sister-in-law, Sabrina Laura. Sabrina was an inspector with the Nice police department. She was a raven-haired beauty in her mid-thirties and mother to four young daughters. She was a charming conversationalist and volunteered to select the perfect Nice lunch for us. We feasted on salade nicoise, petits farcis and ratatouille. The French are truly masters in the kitchen. A locally produced Rose' was the perfect pairing with our elegant meal. "Did you like my choices?" Sabrina asked.

"They were perfect Sabrina, merci beaucoup," I replied.

After lunch Jacques excused himself to care for his children who were back in Cannes with their grandmere. Thibaut, Sabrina, Ace and I joined in the celebratory stroll along the Promenade des Anglaise, a popular beachside walkway. There were two military police visible on every corner and several posted in the middle of the walkway with dogs.

It was a holiday for the French to celebrate their unity and many families were reveling in the happiness of the day. Young and old alike filled the promenade on this sunny day as they took in the sights and sounds of the idyllic seaside setting. As we walked back towards our car, I commented,

"You Frenchmen really know how to live. You stop and smell the roses along the way."

"Yes we do," replied Sabrina.

At that precise moment, mass hysteria broke out. A cargo van plowed into the fun-loving crowd mowing down men women and children in its path of destruction and terror. Panic set in and massive chaos ensued. The French police who were in heavy presence quickly began their assault on the driver of the van who was firing randomly into the innocent crowd. We spotted a second suspicious vehicle rapidly approaching; it appeared to be a back up for the cargo van. The four of us immediately piled into Sabrina's police car, as Ace and I drew our weapons, Sabrina proceeded to pursue the second van, lights and sirens blaring. Thibaut, the ultimate civilian was now in for the ride of his life. An incredible high-speed chase began. Sabrina proved herself to be no stranger to the streets of Nice but even she was frustrated by the 80 mile an hour chase that was endangering not only us but many bystanders along the way. The chase led us to the famous Corniche Roads of the French Riviera. These cliff roads have an abundance of hairpin bends, making them extremely treacherous at high speeds.

Sabrina was experienced on these cliff roads, but the driver of the target vehicle wasn't so adept. He plunged off the Corniche into a deep ravine. Upon impact a massive explosion of flames erupted into the air, black smoke billowed upward to the top of the ravine. The driver must have been carrying a massive amount of explosives to finish off the job his fellow jihadist started back on the Promenade. Luckily on our end of the chase, no one was injured except for the suicidal driver later identified as a 23-year-old Tunisian born Mouez Lajmi. ISIS claimed responsibility for the sadistic attack on Bastille Day. They killed hundreds of innocents: far too many were children. These savages have no respect for human life! Unfortunately, as it turned out, Ace's mole's information was spot on. It just goes to show how difficult it is to prevent such attacks. It's a guarantee from now on in Nice, motor vehicles will be prohibited access to any and all roadways where people are congregating.

The cargo van driver was ultimately shot and killed, but not before inflicting huge carnage, killing 87 people and injuring almost 200 more. We were thankful that we had a part in stopping the terrorist in the second van otherwise the tally could have been much higher. Later that evening, back in Cannes at the hotel, Ace, Thibaut and I had drinks to calm our oh-so frayed nerves.

The next day before we departed for the US, we enjoyed a wonderful meal at C' est Si Bon Restaurant located in Onorine Deux. We spotted actress Jolly Jones a few tables away from us. Jolly was dining with several of her rambunctious children. I guess since her split from husband, Beckett Pratt, she no longer has him around to help quiet them down. C'est la vie!

Thibaut pointed out a lively table of three young beautiful women from Monte Carlo. He identified them as the Grandasse sisters, Giselle, Gabrielle and Gigi Grandasse. The sisters are the stars of their own reality show, *Les Anges Grandasse*. The sisters allow cameras to shadow every move of their very glamorous lives. The French cannot get enough of them. We Americans have our own TV sisters back in the States that Americans just can't seem to get enough of either. I guess we are all more alike than we think.

After Ace and I returned to the U.S.A., it was confirmed that Mustafa Salib was indeed heavily involved in planning the Nice attack. The French police confiscated several computers, cell phones, high powered rifles, ammo, plot notes and maps from the homes of the attackers. Mustafa's involvement was clearly documented as well. Unfortunately, our relentless search will have to continue for Mustafa Salib.

Chapter Ten

Tyra and I were assigned to the investigation of a virtual kidnapping scam
that's been reported by several victims in our jurisdiction. Virtual
kidnapping is an extortion scheme, perpetrated by callers, demanding
ransom in exchange for the release of a loved one. Unlike traditional
kidnappings, virtual abductors haven't taken anyone. Instead, through a
series of deceptions and threats, they coerce the victim to pay a ransom very
quickly. Time is of the essence in this complex racket. All transactions
must be completed before the victim realizes that no actual abduction has
taken place. A call came in on the DA's hot line giving an address in South
Yonkers where the scam originated. The tipster said that the ring-leader is a
Middle Eastern guy by the name of Mustafa Salib. According to the
informant, Salib is using the money to further his jihadist activities. All we
had was Salib's name and nothing else.

Tyra and I arrived on Carroll Street, a commercial/residential neighborhood
in South Yonkers. The tipster mentioned that the guys working the virtual
kidnapping scam were using an apartment on the second floor of a five-
story residence. We planned to surveil the building, observe the foot traffic
in and out and possibly identify people of interest. I turned on the police
portable radio; I listened to the non-stop chatter from the detectives in the
field. Tyra picked up the Canon Telephoto Zoom Lens camera and hung it
around her neck, waiting for the opportunity to snap a photo. Occasionally
peeking over at her as we conversed, I couldn't help but think how
gorgeous she is. If it wasn't for Denise, I'd be in big trouble right now.
About two hours into the surveillance, Tyra shifted her body in the seat,
moving closer to me. I noticed her lustful smile. "Frank, we really need to
seriously catch up." She slowly put her hand on my shoulder. I grabbed
her hand and pulled it away. I was distracted by the sight of a young girl
entering the building. She was in her early twenties, with sandy brown hair,
dressed slovenly in yoga pants and a hooded sweatshirt. "Look Tyra," I
said sharply, "if we're gonna work together we really gotta keep this on a

professional level. Okay? Did you snap a picture of the girl that just walked into the building?"

"What girl?"

"C'mon," I said, as I slowly burned inside because of her lack of attention. "We're here to do a job."

"Sorry," she replied. She was embarrassed and turned away and said, "If she comes out, I'll get the shot." Another twenty minutes passed before the girl staggered out. She was definitely high on something and strung out. Tyra snapped a few pictures of her. My eyes followed the girl staggering down the street until she was out of sight. After 5 hours, we discontinued our surveillance, to be continued on another day.

Chapter Eleven

The four agencies that scoured the bomb scene at Mike's front entrance were unable to collect any incriminating evidence. They hoped to examine what remained of the pipe bomb and connect the findings to one of the bomb makers who were already on their radar. Each bomb maker has his own unique signature. Unfortunately, no connection was made.

I was on my way into the office, mulling over all that happened in the last few days. The attempted kidnapping of Denise and the lack of progress in identifying the perpetrators in my case kept me up at night. I have a long list of people who would like to see me dead. My list of suspects includes Nick Galgano, Ayman Hani and Michael Calise. Hani is about to be released from prison. Galgano and Calise are serving life sentences because of me. Talk about motive!

No one deserves life in jail more than Nick. He's a cold-blooded killer. I was introduced to Nicky "Blue Eyes" by Freddy Spina about 6 years ago. His favorite pastime was breaking legs for Luchese Capo Michael Calise. Calise is another guy who'd like to drink my blood. Calise and Galgano tested me daily for almost a year before I was accepted into the crew.

There were two things that Nicky loved more than life itself, money and his only child Cindy. After Cindy's mother died of brain cancer some years ago, Cindy took care of her father. This changed to some extent when Mike Baraka entered her life and they moved in together. The bad blood between Nick and Mike escalated; on one occasion Nick pistol whipped Mike so badly that he spent a week in the hospital nursing a concussion.

The thought of whoever tried to kill me being somewhere out there has me sleeping a lot less at night; leading to tossing and turning, borderline paranoia, possibly minus the borderline part. This was made ultra apparent when I pulled a gun on sweet old Mrs. O'Grady in the local fruit market as I was searching the perfect Golden Delicious apple. I felt something press against my back. I spun and pulled out my gun like Quick Draw McGraw, only to find the poor old woman trying to help me out by handing me a ripe, spherical specimen of an apple. As I apologized she just looked at me petrified with fresh apple juice dripping all over her blouse from the now crushed apple in her hand. I literally won't get a good night's sleep again until I find out who is trying to kill me.

As I continued to my office, I stopped at one of the red lights on the parkway and noticed a black Lincoln in my rear view mirror. For several days I noticed it following behind me at a distance and then break off. It was playing cat and mouse games with me. On a prior occasion I noticed the car had a deep rust dent in the trunk. I needed to get a look at the car's trunk to see if it's the same one.

I changed lanes; the Lincoln changed lanes behind me. Thanks to Freddy Spina, I'm the best at picking up a tail. I pulled into the passing lane and sped up, passing three or four cars. I kept looking into the rearview mirror. The Lincoln also veered into the passing lane and accelerated. I was completely engaged in the moment as my adrenaline kicked in. I thought, here I go again. They missed me with the bomb, now they're gonna try to finish the job. I could feel my heart in my throat. At least my head wasn't throbbing. Fuck 'em. I'm prepared for the worst. Let's get this shit over with. I pulled my 9mm from under my sweatshirt and placed it on the seat next to me. I'd see what their next move was. I swung the wheel hard and pulled off the parkway. I had the gun in my hand, ready to rock-n-roll. I rolled down the window and waited. The Lincoln blew past me, continuing northbound. A large rusty dent on the trunk caught my eye. I pushed the window up. I waited to calm down before edging out onto the roadway. Baraka's building was just around the corner. I thought I'd swing by to see the damage the bomb had caused to the building. The car with the rusty dent on the trunk was double-parked in front of Mike's building. I parked at the top of the hill, I attempted to get the plate number, but I was too far away.

Mike drove past me, pulling up to the Lincoln. He got out of his car and made a bee-line to the Lincoln. He was extremely animated, engaged in what appeared to be a heated conversation. After a few minutes, the car slowly pulled away. Mike stood on the sidewalk for a minute, as he watched the carpenters install the new set of double doors. He then quickly hustled past them into the five-story walk-up. I waited a minute or so before backing up my car onto Maple Street. I surmised that Mike was up to something, but what? It didn't make any sense. Why was he meeting with whomever was in the Lincoln? This knocked me for a loop. Should I question him about it? No, I thought, I'd keep it to myself until I'd have a better gauge on things. Maybe it will all shake out by itself. Knowing Mike, he's always ahead of the curve.

As soon as I entered the squad room the Captain asked me into his office. Captain C.J. Matthews was recently assigned by Chief Christopher to head up the Narcotics Squad. He's a good cop, with a great reputation for integrity and hard work. One of the brightest and most well-liked bosses in the department, he's been in several righteous shootings and definitely is someone you'd want watching your back on the street. He's a bulldog, once he sinks his teeth into an investigation, he doesn't let go. C.J. is a legend in his own time.

"Hey Cap," I said as I walked in.

"Hey Frankie," he said in his usual up-beat tone of voice, "Grab a chair."
"Cap," I said, shaking my head in frustration, "I was on my way in and noticed that I was being followed by a black Lincoln Continental. It has been behind me now for a few days. I know it's the same car because of a rust dent in the trunk. I pulled over on the parkway, but they sped past me."

"Did ya get a look at em?"

"No, the car had tinted windows, couldn't see who the hell it was."

I made it a point to fill him in on Mike's visit from the FBI. He murmured something under his breath and then said with angst, "FBI, huh. Ya know, I don't have to tell you they stick their nose into everything. Maybe I'll have Nulligan ride with you for a while."

"Nulligan? Sure. By the way, thanks for assigning Pete and John to take care of Denise. We'll have some peace of mind."

Chapter Twelve

Cindy Galgano walked into the Scampi Grill in New York City. She turned a few heads by making a "Dressed to Kill" entrance. Cindy always dressed like she was going out for a night of dancing, even though it was lunch time. You know the type. Big hair, stilettos, spandex, and oversized hoop earrings. Need I say more? You get the picture. Some men find this attractive. I never liked the trashy types. I like good old fashioned class with a capital SEXY. Cindy wanted us to meet in an out of the way place. Here we are.

I stood up to greet her and kissed her on the cheek. Heavy perfume and scent of chocolate invaded my senses. "Smells good, what perfume are you wearing?" I said.

Cindy looked pleased. "Angelic," she replied, "it's my favorite."

We sat and chit-chatted for a bit. Serafina, a Sicilian beauty, took our lunch order. We both had their signature dish, Caprese salad. It's the best. We split a bottle of Pino Grigio. Half way through our meal I said, "So Cindy, the suspense is killing me, why are we meeting like this?" Cindy reached under the table and placed her hand on my knee. After all the wine, we were both feeling loose as a goose.

"Frankie, since the day I met you, you've had a special place in my heart. I admire you for many reasons not the least of which is the way you've helped me and Mike. Mike and I have had our ups and downs. We met and suddenly I'm pregnant with Santino. It was too much, too soon. Mike's lifestyle, plus my dad, it's not all a bed of roses."

"Cindy, I don't know what to say."

"You don't need to say a word, it is what it is."

"Frankie, the other day my father underwent open heart surgery to replace a faulty heart valve. I was at his bedside; just the two of us. He was heavily sedated and was mumbling incoherently. I started a conversation with him. I wasn't sure he could hear me. I told him how much I loved him and that I was sorry I had disappointed him by being with Mike. He appeared to come around a little."

He looked dead in my eyes and said, "Nothing can come between us, baby girl. I got eyes and ears everywhere. Even in the DA's office." He was rambling. I guess the drugs were kicking in. I asked, "What do you mean?"

"I got a guy in my pocket," he whispered.

"At the DA's office?" I asked.

"Yeah," he replied.

"Who?" I asked.

"I pressed him for more information, but he was out cold. He would never have opened up to me like that if he was in his right mind. Believe me," she said.

"Cindy, why are you telling me this?"

"I trust you Frankie. I'm telling you this to protect you. You never heard me say it, capisci? As a matter of fact, we never even met here, that's how it has to be. Mike would blow a gasket if he knew I confided in you. He's terribly possessive," Cindy said in a whisper.

"Does Mike know any of this?" I asked.

"Just you, me and the lamp post," Cindy said. "No, I didn't tell Mike. Santino needs to grow up in a stable home with a mother and father. I'm trying to make that a reality for my son. Mike likes to keep me in a gilded cage but he is a wonderful father to my boy."

"Sorry Cindy. Thanks for trusting me enough to give me this information. It could be life saving. For right now, I'm gonna keep it under wraps. No one will ever know you gave it to me. Somehow, someway, the snitch is going to show his ugly face and I'll be there to put the cuffs on him."

We finished the last of the wine and exited to the parking lot. I escorted Cindy to her white Cadillac SUV. "Take care of yourself Cindy," I said. After an impassioned hug, she drove off. I leaned against my car, taking a few minutes to soak in the new information I had. Now I needed a way to decide what bait to put in the rat trap.

Chapter Thirteen

Early the next morning, I was in the office going over some old files getting reacquainted with Ayman Hani. When he's released from prison, I want to know the places he frequents and the people he hangs with, so I'll know where to start looking for him if he plans on causing me trouble. In addition to Calise and Galgano, Hani has a damn good reason for wanting me dead. Now that he's been radicalized he has an even better reason. I'm an infidel, a non-believer of the tenets of Islam.

Although Michael Calise was Hani's supplier of high-grade heroin, I never ran into him at Calise's social club on Oak Street. Calise and Nick kept their drug dealing away from the social club and usually did business in a low-key hotel in New York City. They knew that the cops had the club under surveillance, so they conducted their drug business at clandestine locations. For that matter, in all the years I spent in Calise's crew, I never ran into Mike Baraka either, even though he lived in the same neighborhood.

As I continued to read through the files, it was apparent that Mike's brother-in-law, Sami Hassan was the go between for the Jordanian Sky Marshals and Calise. Upon landing at JFK Airport, Sami would pick them up and drive to the Holiday Hotel on Queens Blvd. in Jamaica, Queens and engage them in an immediate weight loss program by removing four to eight kilos of heroin that were strapped to their bodies. At times Hani would accompany Sami to meet the Jordanian Sky Marshals.

After the shipment was in Calise's hands, he would portion off some of the heroin to Sami and Hani on consignment to sell. The rest of the shipment would end up in heroin shooting galleries that they ran throughout the New York metropolitan area.

Mike's mother, Adel, was relentless in trying to clear her son's name. She had implored Ayman Hani's mother, her sister Hind, numerous times to help. Adel told Hind that Mike was being punished for a crime that Hind's son Ayman committed and he had suffered enough. Hind had little control of her son but finally she relented. One thing Hind did have was a connection to one of the most respected tribal leaders of the Maayeh, one of the larger Christian tribes in Jordan. His name was Bachir, meaning "Good Tidings."

As a regional tribal elder, Bachir wielded power and commanded respect throughout Jordan. Even in the modern day, to dishonor the tribe was to dishonor all its members. Every tribal member bore shame when another tribal member brought disgrace upon the tribe. Ayman Hani had committed the cardinal sin of allowing another to assume his debt to society, distancing himself from his family and operating outside the dictates of the tribe.

Bachir could not let this stand and told Hind that he would take care of the matter. Bachir then assigned ten or so of his fellow tribesmen to go into the seedier parts of Amman to explain tribal etiquette to Ayman. These were no ordinary tribesmen in Maayeh robes, these were battle-hardened soldiers in the Jordanian army who had experience fighting Jihadists and Al Qaeda terrorists in the desert. They told Hani that if he wasn't on a flight to New York within a week, he would be taken out to the desert in a military transport, tortured and shot. They also advised him that if he didn't follow through with his agreement once in the U.S. they would follow him to the ends of the earth to exact vengeance.

Hani returned to the States, and I took his confession. He was sentenced to serve the time that Mike had been unjustly punished with. Now, after the fact, Hani might want revenge at my expense.

Nulligan yelled out, "Frankie, Tyra's on line 1."

Tyra was settled into her month to month furnished rental in Rye, New York. It was neat, clean and she loved it. It was within walking distance to Purchase Street, one of the quaintest shopping areas in Westchester County. "Hey good looking, what's cooking?" I said.

"Frankie, my landlady, Millie, knows I'm a cop. She's very upset. She just called me from T.D's Smoke shop on Purchase Street where she works. Millie said that her sister's daughter, Andrea, may be a kidnapping victim. Can you meet me at my apartment ASAP?"

"Give me twenty minutes. I'm on my way." I must have broken every traffic law in the book. I was thinking about Tyra, on the drive there. Her work ethic was amazing. She threw herself into every assignment high heeled feet first and gave it her all. Now we'll see how this one shakes out. I arrived at Tyra's place on Smith Street, just in time to see her talking to a uniformed Rye cop. She introduced me to the officer as she continued to discuss the kidnapping of her landlady's niece, Andrea.

"My landlady just left for her sister's house," Tyra said. "She spoke to Sgt. Mc Andrews from the Rye PD before she left. I got all the information we need. Jump in my car Frankie, I told Millie we'd meet her at her sister's house."

"Yes sir," I replied. We both chuckled.

We arrived at the home of Millie's sister, Fran Bancroft, on Langeloh Court in Rye Brook, New York. Lush gardens surrounded a mid-century structure. It looked to be around 10,000 square feet.

Fran and Millie were both crying. Fran greeted us and began to relive her morning's nightmare. "Very early this morning I got a phone call on my cell phone," Fran said. "The first thing I heard was a girl's voice yelling frantically, "Help me!" Next, a man said, "We have your daughter. If you ever want to see Andrea again, listen carefully." Fran broke into sobs and couldn't continue speaking.

"Did it sound like Andrea?" I asked.

"I couldn't really tell," Fran sobbed.

We had no way of knowing if Andrea had been kidnapped, or was it a case of virtual kidnapping. The con artist uses social media to find out all they can about their potential target and their family. If they are cunning enough, they can convince most terror filled family members to see things their way. They may use a recorded voice of a person begging for help. The family is obviously upset after hearing the recorded voice, then panic and the terms of the victim's release follows. The perps usually have enough information to make their ruse plausible.

"He said he had Andrea tied up in a truck and had her cell phone. If I called her cell phone or the police, it would jeopardize her life."

"Then the line went dead," Fran said. "I've left a few messages with her roommates but I cannot find out where my daughter is."

Suddenly the phone rang. "Hello." Fran put the call on speaker. "Is my daughter alright? Please let me talk to her," Fran begged.

"You need to stay on the phone with me." The caller's voice was rough. "No cops or she gets killed. Do you understand? I want $20,000 cash within the next hour. Go to the bank, get the money. Stay on the phone with me and I'll give you more instructions." The man spoke with a foreign accent, possibly Middle Eastern.

Fran panicked. She looked at us frantically. We remained completely silent in order to protect her. I scribbled a note that we would follow her to the bank, at a safe distance. I jotted down my cell number as well.

We tailed her to the local Community Bank. She withdrew $20,000 in large bills. As she exited the bank, a tall person covered from head to toe in a hijab, approached Fran and yanked the purse off Fran's shoulder. Then the woman ran like Satan himself was chasing her. She ran into a nearby alley. On foot, Tyra and I caught up to her. As I tackled her, the purse fell to the ground. The money spilled out onto the walkway. During the tussle, the face covering was removed and revealed that it wasn't a woman after all. It was a bearded man. The man continued to struggle, punching and kicking at Tyra and me. I was finally able to force one of his arms up behind his back so hard, his shoulder popped, dislocating it. He let out a blood curdling yell. Tyra threw her handcuffs on him as he yelped in pain.

After getting him medical attention for his dislocated shoulder, we took him back to the DA's Office for questioning. He said that his name was Nadir Raza, but that's all he would say. He would have to be vetted with the Feds to find out who he really is. We later found out that Raza was in the country illegally. He was turned over to the US Immigration and Customs Service (ICE) for immediate deportation, sending him back to his native Syria. We couldn't prove he was connected to the same operation run out of the apartment on Carroll Street in Yonkers but we had our suspicions. Mustafa Salib's name surfaced as the mastermind behind the scam.

As things turned out, Andrea was never abducted. She was safe and sound traveling to London on a sudden business trip. Fran, although worse for wear, was thrilled that her four hour ordeal was over. She was very grateful to me and Tyra and called us saints.

Chapter Fourteen

Just as Tyra and I walked into the squad room, Nulligan yelled out, "Frankie you got a collect call from an inmate at the Westchester County Jail."

"Frank, it's Peter, Peter Falcone," he said sounding a bit anxious. "I'm sure you remember me." Pete peddled cocaine but he sold it to the wrong guy and got himself arrested. He worked as my C.I. (Confidential Informant) for awhile, until he satisfied his beef and avoided the joint.

"Hey, Pete. I guess you fucked up again?" I said with a subtle snicker. Unfortunately, Pete's addicted to heroin and is in the slam again for selling drugs to another undercover cop. Now, he's looking for some help. The problem is that Pete is now a predicate felon, which means he's had a number of felony arrests and convictions and the court has no choice but to sentence him to time in state prison. After I had initially arrested Pete, he decided to work for me and stay out of jail; he introduced me to a mid-level Dominican drug dealer from Washington Heights, in upper Manhattan. I passed myself off as a wise guy, looking for a new cocaine connection. I was able to get over on the goofball and score seven kilos of almost pure cocaine from the unsuspecting mope. He was sentenced to prison for twenty-five years. It was a big case for me, got me recognized by the bosses in the office, ultimately advanced my career.

Falcone reached out thinking that he could worm his way out of going to state prison by giving me another big case. He has some Intel on his cell mate, says the guy is looking for a hit man to murder a state witness that is going to testify against him. Believe it or not, this happens a lot. Many a conviction has been obtained from an inmate who's looking for a get out of jail free card by testifying against a cellmate. Although Pete was a distraction from finding who's responsible for turning my life up-side down, he was like so many drug addicts who end up in prison or dead.

After a brief conversation, Pete knew that I was on board with helping him. His tone changed and he sounded relieved. The phone went silent for a few seconds. I guess he was mulling over his situation. There was a chance that he might not have to serve the remainder of his young life in state prison. I had to finally say something. "Ah, you all right? You there?"

"Um... yeah. I'm here. Just thinking," he said.

I had to lay out a game plan. "Pete, tell your cellmate that you know a street guy who can take care of his problem and make it go away. I need to know all about the dirt-bag. So what's the guy's name and what's he in for?"

"Frankie, he's Iranian. His name is Wal Azizi. He nearly beat his cousin Khalid to death with a baseball bat because Khalid held out on him on a coke deal." Not surprising, I thought, typical thug behavior. Wal Azizi doesn't want to do any serious jail time. He'd rather have his cousin murdered and walk free.

"Alright," I said, "have him call me collect tomorrow, after 5 p.m." I gave him my confidential number to get the ball rolling.

"Frank I can't do time in state prison," Pete said stammering. "Thanks." The phone clicked off. I ran back into Captain Matthews's office and briefed him on the call. He told me to make sure to bring Beau Winslow up to speed. Beau Isaac Winslow is a young aggressive attorney who has been working in the DA's office for five-years. A graduate from Brooklyn Law School, Beau graduated at the top of his class. He's tall, blond and handsome. Some say he made a mistake going into law. He should have gone to Hollywood and tried his hand at acting. Beau would be handling any legal issues that come up in the investigation.

Chapter Fifteen

Our newly elected DA John Xavier Hogan, thirty eight, graduated from Georgetown Law School in the top 5% of his class. He's a born leader and his handsome, dignified appearance only promotes his popularity. Prior to his election he was General Counsel for the U.S. Security and Exchange Commission in Washington, D.C.

He married into a politically connected family when he wed J.C. Rollins, daughter of John Rollins, former Governor of Texas. J.C. is a former fashion editor of Elle Magazine. Whenever John and J.C. enter a room all eyes are on them. They are the chic Ken and Barbie power couple that have the best public relations team this side of the Rockies. They are ever present in the press as a couple on the go, doing good work both professionally and personally.

J. X. Hogan is a young rising star who aspires to climb the political ladder to the top rung. Everyone in the DA's office is proud to be on his winning team. Prosecutor Beau Winslow and I had a working breakfast in his office. Bagels and coffee fit the bill. We discussed my recent dealings with Peter Falcone.

"So, Peter Falcone wants some leniency for incriminating Wal Azizi on a murder for hire. Typical jail-house snitch," Beau remarked. "You and I have witnessed our share of them haven't we Frankie."

"We sure have Beau, but the timing of this one could be very important. The Azizi cousins could have some vital information that could lead us closer to the fanatical terror cell," I replied.

"Let's hope so," Hogan said. "We need something to break the case open."

"By the way," Hogan asked, "are you and Beau free to play golf at Winged Foot on Saturday morning? It's a member guest tournament."

Beau and I looked at each other as if to say, "Are you kidding me." We both replied, "We'll make ourselves available."

We made golf arrangements and left Hogan's office. Beau asked me to stop by his office for a minute before heading back to the squad room.

"How is Denise dealing with all the shit, Frank?" Beau asked.

"I'm amazed at how gracefully she's handling it all. She's a trooper," I replied.

"Hey Beau, are you seeing anybody special right now?" I asked. "Denise wanted to fix you up with a friend of hers Haylii, she's a knockout."

"I'm not seeing anyone at all," Beau said. "Last year I fell hard for someone. It was like a thunder bolt hit me. Boom! After some ups and downs, we called it quits. Believe me, it wasn't a simple scenario. I'm like a wounded bear so I'm laying low in the dating world. The truth is between my job and golf, I'm totally booked up."

"Are you sure Beau," I said. "Haylii's hot."

"Frankie, tell Denise maybe down the road," Beau said.
I couldn't help but ask, "Beau, any chance for reconciliation with this mystery woman?"

"You never know," Beau said. "Anything's possible but it looks hopeless. My track record in love isn't so great. You know right after I graduated from Brooklyn Law School I was engaged to a beautiful woman that I had dated for two years. We planned on a future and family together and we were very happy. We were from different religious backgrounds. Her wealthy parents made it their mission in life to break us apart. It's a long story but ultimately they succeeded. The pressure got to my fiancé and she broke it off."

"It was a very dark time for me," Beau continued. "I've shied away from relationships, that is until last year."

"Sorry to hear that Beau," I said. "Maybe things will be brighter in the future."

"Frankie, I take life one day at a time," Beau said. "I look forward to each and every minute and I'm wide open to whatever comes my way."

"I like that attitude, Beau!" I replied.

"Hey," I said. "I've got things to do."

"See ya later Frankie," Beau said. "Let me know how the call from Azizi goes."

"Will do."

Chapter Sixteen

It was a little after seven when I got home. Denise wasn't home yet and the apartment was hauntingly quiet. I pulled off my sweatshirt threw it on the couch and turned on the radio. There was an open bottle of pino grigio on the coffee table. I poured a glass and plopped down on the couch to relax. Finally, I could have a few minutes of peace and calm. I peeled away the bandage on my forehead, felt the small scars and what was left of the stitches. They seemed to be slowly dissolving one by one.

It was after 8:00 p.m. when Denise came home with a bottle of chardonnay tucked under her arm. She wasted no time uncorking it. "I bought a bottle of wine. Pete and John just dropped me off. They're so nice." I heard the cork pop from the kitchen. She strutted back into the living room with the wine and two glasses sitting on a small silver serving tray. She carefully placed it on the coffee table. "Hey," I said, somewhat surprised, "Is there a special occasion or something?"

Her eyes said it all. She moved her hand onto my leg, softly massaging it. With a sultry look she said, "Honey, everyday is a special occasion with you," and grabbed the bottle of chardonnay, filling the two glasses. Our eyes were focused on one another. We raised our glasses and made a lovers toast. I was completely aroused, sparks were flying. I knew we were heading to the bedroom. She put her glass down, drew herself into me, our bodies touching her lips inches away and planted a gentle kiss squarely on my lips. I felt her body go limp. Her eyes centered on mine as she shifted her head back, just enough so that I could still feel her breath on my face. "We'll get through this. Frankie, I love you."

I gently pushed her down onto the couch as she surrendered herself. I kissed her lips as though I could devour her. Articles of our clothing flew all over the room. I passionately undressed her piece by piece. Her body was on fire. As the song lyrics say, *Her body is a wonderland.* Soft moans escaped her mouth as I explored every tantalizing inch of her. Our sexual chemistry was at a fever pitch. She whispered, "Oh Frankie, I love you so very much." I didn't want the pleasure to end but the sexual feeling mounted to such a degree that we were unable to control our passions any longer. As we lay there, exhausted, there was no doubt in my mind that I wanted to share the rest of my life with her. "Denise, I'm totally in love with you. I never had this with anyone else," I said softly. She took hold of my face, kissing me wildly. "Yes, yes Frankie, I know."

Chapter Seventeen

There's a small office with a dedicated phone line, on the fourth floor of the DA's office. That's where incoming calls from bad guys, like Wal Azizi are received and recorded. My pre-recorded greeting is: *"You've reached Frank Miranda. Leave your name, number, time of call, and I'll get back to you."*

At 5 p.m. I was waiting for Azizi to call, but my mind was absorbed in thinking about my love making with Denise last night. We had a thing for one another that made my head spin. I felt like we were in a protective plastic bubble where no one could touch us.

A little after five, the phone rang. The AT&T operator announced there was a collect call from the Westchester County Jail for Frank Miranda. "I'll accept the charges," I said.

"This is Frank." There was a slight pause on the phone.

"Hello Frank. This is Wal Azizi, I'm a friend of Peter Falcone."

"Hey Wal, I've been expecting your call, how ya doin?"

He mumbled something and said, "I've had better days."

Right off the bat I could hear a Middle Eastern accent. I replied bluntly, "I'm sure you've had better days. But listen, ya know we gotta be careful on the phone. They record this shit."

"Yeah, yeah, I know."

Wal was hostile and angry. He said impatiently, "Peter said that you can help me. I'm looking for someone to be, what's the word? Someone to mediate a situation for me."

I could feel the desperation in his voice. "Well, it depends," I said as I tried to reel him in.

"Depends on what?" he said, sounding like he was throwing me a life line.

"On a lot of stuff, my friend. Uh...uh. Where ya from?"

He replied gruffly, "I'm from the Middle East. The Middle East, is that a problem for you?"

"No, no problem. But there's a lot of shit going on over there right now. Ya know. Some of your countrymen are causing problems here."

"Yeah, yeah, I know. The fucking place is on fire. That's why I'm in the US. But look Frank, Peter told me all about you. I need someone to kind of make someone come to their senses, if you know what I mean."

Forcefully, I said, so he'd understand where I was coming from and that I was a serious man. "Look Wal, I'm definitely a problem solver. I can make your problem go away, but we gotta come to some agreement, if you know what I mean?"

"Yeah, yeah, I know exactly what the fuck you mean," he said with an air of arrogance. Game on. I could tell that Wal was comfortable. "I need something to show good faith."

"Good faith? No problem with that Frank, as long as it's taken care of."

I felt that I had him where I wanted him and set the hook in a little deeper. I still needed to sink it in as deep as it would go to keep him in jail for a long, long time. There are a few more scenes in this three act play before he's charged with solicitation to commit murder.

"Ah Wal," I said, "we can work out the details, but I want to see you in person so I can get a better fix on things. When are visiting hours?"

He hesitated, as if he didn't know. In a strained voice he said, "I really don't know but it goes by the inmate's last name."

"Yeah, I'll make a call and find out."

The motor mouth began to talk about his problem and I abruptly cut him off. "Easy, easy my friend, we're on the phone," I snapped.

"Sorry, I understand."

"Wal, our conversations are recorded."

The dirt bag was despondent and at this point completely focused on having me whack his cousin so he could go free. What he didn't know was that he was talking to a cop and that I was recording our conversation. I wanted to keep him talking, but I had to be careful. He was street smart and could smell a cop if I pushed him too hard. I wanted him to feel like I was family. "Ah, huh, Wal. Don't worry. I'm in this with you all the way. When I see you in person, we can talk about everything. I'll need some material from you first, if you know what I mean."

His emotions were on high burner. "Got it," he replied.

"Wal, I don't want to make no fuckin mistakes. The loose ends gotta be tied up."

He nervously spat out, "Yup. You know, as a matter of fact, today, I'll scrape together all the information you need."

"Um let me think. I'm gonna have to have it dropped off.......that's important, let me work on it."

"Yeah, yeah, work on it," I shot back. "Work on getting everything to me, especially five grand up front. Remember once we sit down and agree on what I gotta do, ya know there's no going back. Capisci?"

His voice cracked. "Yeah, yeah," he spat out. "I want to get out of here and get on with my fuckin life."

"I hear you brother," I said in an optimistic tone. "It's an unfortunate situation you're in, but these things happen. They happen every day to people."

"Yeah, I know but it happened to me and me is all I freakin' care about."

I cut him off. "Wal, we'll pick this when I see you. So listen, I'm gonna stop by soon."

"Very good Frank. I won't disappoint you."

"Okay Wal, call me. We'll talk at the same time tomorrow."

I logged our recorded conversation of murder for hire into evidence with Sgt. Steve Skowronski, the supervisor in charge of our Technical Services Squad. I shot the shit with Steve for a minute and then walked out into the squad room expecting to find Nulligan but he'd left already. Tyra was still in the office. She's just finished the report of the virtual kidnapping of her landlady's niece. I asked about the Carroll Street investigation.

"So far, we haven't been able to identify any of the perps working out of the building that run the scam," Tyra said. "We have a huge hunch that drugs are also being sold out of that location."

Tyra looked up at me, smiled and said, "You're working late too? What's up?"

"Yeah, working on a killing for hire case, I'd rather be out there hunting the people that tried to kill me."

"Any leads?" she asked.

"No, not yet," I said with trepidation. "By the way, have you had a chance to have the photos you shot on Carroll Street processed?"

Turning back to her report, she shook her head no and said, "No, not yet. I have to get the memory card to the Tech Squad for downloading."
Joe was at Jake's Bar and Grill wetting his beak. Jake's is a popular watering hole that was cop friendly. I thought I'd stop by and have a few pops before heading home. The thought crossed my mind to ask Tyra, but the ways things are going between us, I figured with a few drinks under our belts, it might not be a good idea. As it turned out, she beat me to the punch. "Frank," she said unemotionally, continuing to bang away on the computer, "Joe said he was stopping by Jake's. Why don't we surprise him?"

"Sounds like a plan."

Chapter Eighteen

Jake's Bar & Grill is located in the Chester Heights section of New Rochelle. The bar was crowded, maybe three deep. You could hear the buzz of good natured chatter as I entered the bar. Jessica, Joe's girlfriend, was tending bar. As soon as she saw me she waved me over. She looked upset. Tyra, sensing that something was up, waited near the entrance of the dining room, so as not to pry.

Jessica Carbone, age 27, is a very pretty woman with a pleasant personality to match. She takes pride in her physical appearance with a daily dose of a rigorous workout at the gym. She puts up with Joe's shit like nobody else would. I guess she loves him. After her alcoholic father Marty Olofson, was arrested for physically abusing Jess 9 and her sister Carol 7, the siblings were separated and tossed from foster home to foster home. Their mother passed away from a heart attack two years after the birth of Carol.

After four traumatic years of being apart the sisters were finally reunited and placed in the foster home of Maria and Croce Carbone, two New York City firefighters. The girls had luckily found their forever home. The four Carbone's were the perfect combination and Maria and Croce wasted little time making the situation permanent, within one year the girls were formally adopted. The Carbone's gave Jess and Carol the love and stability every kid deserves. The girls adore their parents and praise them every chance they get. Jess has said that she could be living on the streets if not for them. They truly saved two wonderful little girls and gave them a home.

"Hey Jess," I said. Jess pointed towards Joe sitting in a back booth. "He's at it again. I can't take much more; it dredges up too many drunken memories of Marty. Please tell him it's time to stop. He's had enough!"

"I can't do that Jess, I've been there myself. It's like the pot calling the kettle black," I replied. I stepped away from the bar to join Tyra.

Jake's is modeled after an old fashioned Irish Pub in Dublin. The interior and exterior of the bar are painted Gaelic green. The bar top is made of a dark cherry wood, with six taps pouring the freshest Irish beer. On the back wall are shelves stocked with the finest selection of Irish whiskeys. At the far end of the bar is an opening to the kitchen for quick access for pub fare. Off the bar is a small dining room, with six tables. Red colored leather backed booths line the wall for more intimate conversations. The owner's son Jake McDonald Jr. is a NYPD cop who works patrol in the 47th precinct in the Bronx. Cops gravitate here naturally.

Joe was chugging a beer as Tyra and I approached him. "Hey guys," he said slurring his words, "grab a seat." We settled in across from him. Joe got the waiters attention by waiving his hand in the air and shouting, "My friends need a drink." The waiter, a young college kid, nodded and gave Joe a thumb up and came right over. Tyra ordered an Apple Martini and I ordered a Dewar's White Label and soda. Joe was definitely three sheets to the wind. His elbows rested on the table top. His words were twisted as he spoke. "Frankie, glad you stopped by. Jess is pissed off at me. She wants to cut me off." I don't know how Tyra felt, but I didn't want to get involved in Joe and Jessica's business. I stopped in to relax and have a drink, that's all.

Jessica came from behind the bar in our direction. She was dressed in her usual garb, jeans, a green tee-shirt, with Jake's Bar & Grill logo. Besides wanting to make Joe feel more miserable than he's already feeling, I'm sure she wanted to meet Tyra and check her out. Joe was too drunk to introduce her, so I took it upon myself to make the introductions. "Jessica, this is Detective Sergeant Tyra Williams, she's here from the Las Vegas PD."

Jessica stuck out her hand and said with a wide smile, "Tyra, it's nice to finally meet you. You're even more beautiful than I've heard."

Joe, now incoherent, hung his head and garbled, "Jess, bring us another round. It's on me." Jessica, not wanting to embarrass him said calmly, "Joey, I'll be finishing up soon. Let's go home."

Joe's eyes were completely shut. He had passed out and was snoring. Jessica tried her best to keep her composure. "Frankie, I think it's time I take him home."

Tyra leaned against my shoulder, whispered in my ear, "Is Joe always like this?"

I just looked at her nodding my head yes and said, "Yeah, he's got a lot of issues; living without his kids for one. His ex-wife is giving him a hard time about seeing his them."

Tyra and I finished our drinks, worked our way through the crowd and out the door. We talked in front of the bar for a while about Joe's drinking problem.

As Tyra was about to get into her car, she invited me for a nightcap at her apartment. "Just a friendly drink, nothing more, really."

Uneasy about her invitation, I replied. "No can do, Tyra. I'll see you in the office tomorrow."

Chapter Nineteen

The air was crisp and sunny on this mid-September morning. I was about to pick up dry cleaning before driving to work and noticed a late model black Lincoln a few cars behind me. Every time I turned around the car was there. My eyes never left the Lincoln as it passed me and headed for the parkway. I decided to see once and for all who was following me. I barreled towards the parkway to catch these wahoos, but they had entered the parkway driving south and were out of my sight.

I continued to drive south on the parkway and spotted the Lincoln about an eighth of a mile ahead of me. I could barely see the rusted dent in the trunk, but it was there. The car veered from the far left lane into the right lane and exited at the Mt. Vernon exit. I turned the wheel hard and followed suit, but was too far behind the car to see where it had gone. I continued to drive around the immediate area, but they'd vanished. Damn!

I arrived in the squad room a bit unsettled from chasing the phantom Lincoln. Joe was at his desk, nursing a hangover. The thought of writing a report at the moment didn't sit well with me. I know that Joe had to feel the same way. Nevertheless, what transpired the previous day had to be put into a police report, so I began to bang away on my keyboard. Between the pressure I was under and the noise in the squad room, it was hard for me to concentrate.

Angel Serrano was on the phone screaming at his lawyer about his ex-wife breaking his balls because he was late with this month's child support and how she was about to take him to family court. This forty year old, bilingual, baby faced detective can hold his own anywhere, anytime, with anyone. When it comes to dealing with snitches, he's the best there is. He'd grown up on the mean streets of the South Bronx and he knew how to handle himself in the ghetto.

His parents moved from Puerto Rico when he was ten and he had learned how to survive on the streets, at the same time keeping out of serious trouble, due to a strict upbringing his parents enforced. Short and wiry, with an aggressive personality, like Joe, Angel has a short fuse. I'm sure that his lawyer is aware of that now.

Angel's ex-wife of fifteen-years initiated the divorce. Jenny was on a trip to Puerto Rico last year to visit her parents; she hooked up with an old lover and they rekindled their flame. Before Jenny knew it she was pregnant and decided to come clean with Angel. She plans on living back in Puerto Rico and taking Angel's kids with her. He's heartbroken but still manages to be one of the best cops I know. The ladies love his Latino good looks and he is a charmer. He hopes to find love again this time with someone faithful.

I don't know what it is, but divorce seems to be a disease that comes with the job. For cops, the late nights, the drinking after work and the pressures to take care of your family all contribute to a this dilemma. More than 50% of the guys in the detective division were divorced and drank too much, myself included.

Besides the hangover, Joe looked dejected and said, "Did ya hear? Looks like another Inspector's funeral. I can't wait to fuckin' retire so I don't have to attend another cop's funeral." As I squeezed behind him to sit down, I replied, "Yeah, I heard on the radio. He leaves behind a wife and a three year old daughter, very sad."
As I entered the report of my recorded telephone conversation with Wal Azizi, I got my mind prepared for my actual meeting with him in the Westchester County Jail. Like a professional athlete preparing for a game, the butterflies immediately go away when you hear the whistle, signal the start of the game.

Chapter Twenty

I was staring at the clock anxiously waiting for Wal Azizi to call. Have you noticed how time seems to stands still when you're waiting for something to happen? It must be part of the human condition. When the hour and minute hand struck exactly 5:00 p.m. the phone rang.

He sounded upset and impatient. "Um, I'm just um, you know apprehensive. I'd really like to get together with you and get this thing moving along."

I replied, "Yeah, me too. I'm planning to come up Friday night."

His tone immediately changed, he sounded a bit relieved. I was his get out of jail free card. He responded, "Beautiful Frank, beautiful." Anxiously he said, "When I'm out of here, we need to sit down. I got more work for you. A few competitors, ya know?"

I wanted to make sure that there were no misgivings about what he wanted me to do. I wanted every word that came out of his mouth to be on tape. "We'll iron everything out on Friday night but before I come up I want the five large. We clear?"

Wal was so pumped up! He began to ramble on, not making any sense.

"Wal, calm down, we gotta be clear on how things go."

"Okay Frank. Okay. I got everything in place for you. You can pick up the things you need tomorrow," he said, in his quest for freedom. I was a heartbeat away from having Wal in my back pocket. Once I picked up the five grand, he could forget about seeing the light of day for a long, long, time. I'm thinking the upside on all this is that I'll get to have a heart to heart talk with his cousin Khalid. When his cousin finds out that Wal put a hit out on him, just maybe, he'll want to cooperate. Wal said, "Frank, do you know the Enrico's Bar? It's on the corner of 32nd Street and Park Avenue South in Manhattan."

"Yeah, I've heard of it," I said gruffly. Wise guys have been known to hang there. It's kinda unusual for Arabs to go to the place.

"Ya know, don't worry, I'll have everything there for you tomorrow," he said. "A friend will leave the money in an envelope with Louie, the day bartender. It'll have your name on it. Go in and pick it up."

I grumbled, warning him, "This friend of yours better know how to keep his mouth shut."

He stuttered as if he was unsure that his friend would come through for him, and said emphatically, "I....I....Fra...Frank, I trust this guy with my life."

"You'd better trust him, remember Wal, it's my life too."

Chapter Twenty-One

Enrico's Bar is in a busy neighborhood, with a lot of foot traffic on the avenue. I arrived at 2:00 p.m. I looked around briefly to get the lay of the land. I swung open the dark brown weather-beaten door of this flea-bag bar and entered the dimly lit shit-hole. I'm sure blood and guts have been spilled in the joint when one or more of the degenerates who hang in the place had too much to drink. Three beer-chugging unsavory characters lined the bar. They were dressed in dirty work clothes and talking about last nights Yankee game. I interrupted them and said to the bartender, "I'm looking for Louie."

The bartender had a dubious look on his face and shot back. "I'm Louie, what's it to ya?" The short fat knobby headed fuck was dressed like a swamp rat, who hadn't bathed in weeks. He took an aggressive posture and answered, "Who the fuck wants to know?" as he snapped his red suspenders.

"Frank Miranda. Ya got something for me?" I said as I leaned against the bar.

When Louie opened his big mouth again, I noticed the plaque on his teeth was so thick you'd need an ice-pick to remove it. He picked up a dirty glass from the slop sink under the bar and glared at me as he scrubbed it with a scrub brush. "Yeah, I got somethin' here." The guys at the bar seemed uneasy as he reached under the bar and pulled out a rolled up newspaper. Damn, I've been in more comfortable situations.

I didn't want to waste any more time with the bloated fuck. "Give it to me," I said vehemently. Like the cretin was doing me a fucking favor, he reluctantly handed it to me. I quickly unrolled the newspaper and peeked inside. There was a manila envelope with my name printed in large black letters in the middle. It contained a small wad of money, papers and a photograph.

Louie grabbed the empty glasses sitting in front of the bar-rats and filled them with beer from the tap. He turned to me, asking, "How do you know Wal?"

I leaned forward, resting my hand on the bar, replying, "That's none of your business." I raised my chin, nodding to him and the three scumbags and put the envelope in my breast pocket, turned around and walked out. In my car, I opened the envelope and pulled out a stack of twenties and counted it. It was $5,000. There was a photo of Khalid Azizi and his address.

The next step was to meet with Wal on Friday night. Now that I finally had the 5k in my hot little hands, Wal's fate was sealed.

Chapter Twenty-Two

Tyra and Joe were growing weary of their surveillance gig on Carroll Street. We knew the action was on the second floor, but exactly which apartment was unknown. At the moment, obtaining a search warrant was our highest priority. Standard operating procedure was to have an informant make a drug buy which gave us probable cause to search the apartment.

In order to obtain the search warrant, probable cause must be established. Enter Jack Aloysius Bolster. Jack was Joe's C.I. of choice for this game of cat and mouse. Jack looks like one of the irredeemable characters in "Breaking Bad." His junkie mother was responsible for his dismal prospects in life. Were it not for The Little Sisters of the Poor, he might be dead. The Sisters run a small shelter on East 146th Street in the South Bronx. They are dedicated to helping the zombies who roam the streets in search of finding their next fix. A wealthy Catholic benefactor, who lost a child to the opioid epidemic, generously donated the small house to their charity. They operate "St. Augustine's House" on continued funding from the benefactor Judith Lee, a former Bronxite now living in Johns Island, Vero Beach, Florida. They're all saints!

Bolster was told to enter the building at the same time as one of the living dead and shadow him to the apartment to make a narcotics buy. He was given $200.

Joe told me that he and Tyra had become very comfortable with each other in the last few days. They were spending countless hours cooped up in the car on the surveillance. They began to confide in each other. Joe told Tyra he really needed to get control of his drinking habits. Too many trips to Jake's were taking their toll. In turn Tyra told Joe about her ex-boyfriend, Chad Kane. Tyra met him at a wine tasting in Vegas. Chad was born into a well-to-do family of Napa Valley vintners. At first Tyra enjoyed the lavish lifestyle Chad introduced her to. Golf at Pebble Beach, dinners at

Morimoto Napa, weekends spent on the Baja Peninsula. Chad was enamored with the idea that he was dating a female detective.

Gradually, Tyra could feel his possessive nature surface. After six months of dating, she broke it off. This enraged Chad. He set out on a mission to make her life miserable. He stalked her every move. Tyra was forced to get a restraining order against him. A few of her colleagues had a heart to heart with Chad. It did the trick.

In deepest confidence, Joe also told me that Tyra told him a tale that set him back on his heels. A few nights ago, on her way home, she stopped for a drink at the Stag's Head Pub in Rye. There was an overflow crowd. She found a seat at the bar and ordered Blanton's Bourbon neat. A few sips in, she began to mellow. Lo and behold, Chief Larry Christopher walked through the door. He spotted Tyra and made a direct beeline toward her. "Chief, what brings you to this part of town?"

"Ah....I was just in the neighborhood and decided to stop for a drink."

Larry asked the bartender for another round for Tyra and a Clan MacGregor scotch on the rocks for himself. Larry smiled and said, "If you haven't eaten yet, let's grab a booth."

"Sounds great Chief," she replied, "I'm starved."

Tyra slid into a small booth near the back of the restaurant. The chief boldly slid in next to her. "You look beautiful, Tyra. You always do," Larry said.

Stunned, Tyra remained silent. They ordered off the menu as Tyra struggled to keep the conversation on a professional level. As the evening progressed the chief was heavy-lidded and was slurring his words. The waiter delivered her turkey club and his Reuben sandwich.

Larry moved his hand onto Tyra's thigh. She jolted away with what little space she had. His bloodshot eyes were fixed on hers. "Tyra don't make a scene. I can make things very bad for you at work."

Tyra said that she tried to say something, but Larry put his forefinger to her lips and shushed her. He then said, "The first time I laid eyes on you, I wanted you. Let's go back to your apartment."

Tyra had enough and literally shoved Larry out of the booth and bolted out of the place. Since that night, the chief has been harassing her with calls and sexting messages. Tyra said that she doesn't know what to do, or what her next step is. She doesn't want to bring the matter to the DA, but she will have to make a decision soon as to how to handle it. She didn't want to ruin Larry's life due to these transgressions.

Joe and Tyra's conversation ended when Jack Bolster left the building. He walked around the corner to Riverdale Avenue and met up with them outside. Joe was parked at the curb in a Pontiac Firebird. Bolster was all smiles and handed Joe a small tin foil package and said, "Heroin. I followed the guy right to apartment 2F. I copped from a couple of Arabs."

We now had the probable cause to search apartment 2F for drugs.

Chapter Twenty-Three

A no-knock search warrant was issued for Carroll Street. Joe and Tyra approached the apartment door. Joe wielded a battering ram to bust open the steel door. One or two direct hits to the door lock usually does the trick, for a guy with Joe's strength, one good strike did it.

They rushed into the small dark apartment with high power flash lights braced under their pistols. No one was in the living room but as they entered the bedroom a long, lean bearded man was in their sights. He was wearing a floor length white night gown and holding a young girl in front of him as a human shield. He held a pistol to her head. The girl was sobbing and looked terrified as they backed up to the window. Little did the bearded one know that Angel and I had positioned ourselves on the fire escape of the bedroom, we flanked each side of the window hiding out of sight. Angel motioned to me that he had a clear shot and pulled the trigger, instantly killing the man. The girl fell to the floor and instinctively crawled her away from the body in hysterics. Tyra handcuffed her and did her best to try to calm her down.

A thorough search of the apartment yielded information about the virtual kidnappings. A notebook with a list of victims and $100,000 in cash along with over two kilos of uncut heroin were found.

The decedent, Anaan Khadum from Turkey was on the FBI's terrorist watch list. News of his death will put his terrorist cell on high alert. As customary, forensics will analyze laptops and computers seized from the apartment.

The girl was taken to an interrogation room at the DA's office. She said her name was Hannelore Vissor. She was about five feet-two inches tall and bone thin. Hannelore appeared to be about 15-years old; although she insisted she was nineteen. She had no I.D., so it was impossible to verify any of what she said. She claimed to have been living in Oudewater, a small town in the Netherlands. Eighteen months ago, she and a friend travelled to Bruges, Belgium for a holiday trip. Hannelore said, "After dinner one evening, my friend Nina and I went dancing at Club Bruges. We met some guys there who drugged and kidnapped us. We woke up handcuffed in a van and we were transported to Istanbul and sold as sex slaves. I never saw Nina again. I was given a new identity and fake passport. I ended up being the personal property of that monster you killed today. He beat, starved and raped me several times a day. It was a living hell. Please, when can I go home?"

"Hannelore, we first have to verify all this and then we'll deal with your logistics," Tyra said.

"Please, you can contact my uncle Hans Valckenier, he's the mayor of Oudewater. I'm sure my disappearance has been in the news."

As it turned out, Hannelore Vissor was telling the truth. She was released and returned to her home in the Netherlands for a joyful reunion with her family. The search continues for her missing friend Nina.

Sex trafficking is a booming industry and a global threat. We were proud that we ended the misery of at least one nineteen year old.

Chapter Twenty-Four

My lucky brown suit. What I'm about to tell you may sound eccentric but I
suppose we all have our superstitions. Mine involves a medium weight
brown worsted wool suit. So far the rosary beads that Mike's mother Adel
gave me and the suit haven't failed me. They keep me safe. I wear the suit
when my persona needs to be a savvy street smart wise guy.

The Westchester County Correctional Facility is cold and dismal. My
meeting with Wal Azizi was to take place in the dayroom, a secure
controlled environment. I thought it wouldn't hurt if I wore my lucky
brown suit. I'd be wearing a wristwatch, with a digital audio voice recorder
embedded to record our conversation.

I arrived at the facility at 6:30 p.m. I turned on the digital recorder and
walked over to the visitor's entrance. A female corrections officer was
seated in a booth behind the plexi-glass window. She asked to see my
driver's license and who I was visiting. She slid the visitor's log through a
slot at the bottom of the window for my signature. I was escorted, along
with other visitors, to a massive gate with floor to ceiling steel bars. The
gate was controlled electronically by another officer from a room on the
other side of the wall. Once inside, we were accompanied down a long,
dark, depressing corridor to an x-ray machine. I took everything out of my
pockets and placed the stuff in a small plastic tray. Fortunately my wrist
watch went through the machine without a hitch. They're looking for
contraband, like weapons and narcotics. I distinctly remember a feeling of
isolation because of the sheer harshness of the place. I could actually feel a
lump in my throat and a sense that the walls were closing in on me as I
approached the visitor's room. I gave my lucky brown suit a rub. I asked
the officer, a large male with a goatee, to point out Azizi. He raised his arm
and pointed across the room, to a male in his late twenties, seated at a table
bolted to the floor. Wal was not a looker, he had several large moles on his
cratered face, his neck tats were several blue snakes, and he wore his hair in

a man bun. He looked across the day room as I stood in the doorway. Our eyes met and he knew instinctively who I was. "Frank, I'm Wal Azizi. It's nice to meet you." He studied every inch of me, cleared his throat and said, "Oh, by the way, nice suit."

I chuckled to myself and said, "Never leave home without it."

We sat and I strategically rested my hands on the table, so as to obtain a clear recording. "Look Wal, you gotta tell me exactly what you want me to do to Khalid. Understand? Once we agree, it's a done deal. There's no turning back."

Wal stared at me as he placed his forefinger under his own chin, drawing it across his neck, indicating that he wanted me to slit Khalid's throat. "I want him dead. I want the motherfucker dead. Nobody, but nobody screws me, not even my cousin."

"He fucked you? How?"

He hesitated for a second, clenching his fists then opening them and said, "Cocaine. He held out on a Coke deal. Like I said, nobody cheats me, Frank. I gotta uphold my reputation on the street."

"I understand," I said. "Street cred is everything."

I was glued on his every movement to see if I was convincing him. I leaned in closer and made a sinister sound. "Wal, I'll drink his fuckin' blood if you want. It's just business, that's all it is to me. You'll read all about it in the newspapers."

Wal's icy smirk was replaced by a cold smile. "That's what I want to hear, I want him fuckin' dead. Ya got it?"

We were so close that I could smell his septic breath. I got a closer look at his teardrop tattoo under his left eye. I growled back and said, "Believe me Wal, I'm everybody's worst fucking nightmare. I'm what bad dreams are made of."

Wal leaned back, cupped his hands and placed them on the table top. His body language said that he was relaxed and knew that his cousin would be dealt with and he'd soon be free.

In a muted tone, I asked, "So what about the other $5,000?"

"As soon as it's done," he said, "there'll be another envelope at Enrico's with five gees in it."

"Trust me, your cousin Khalid ain't gonna show up to testify; remember Wal, I want what's owed me. I can also become your worst enemy too. By the way, you should give Pete Falcone a taste. He set this thing up."

Wal gazed up at me with a look of satisfaction on his face. He beamed as he reached out for my hand. "Like you Italians say, it's only business." Before the door closed behind me, I looked back at Wal sitting there in his orange jump suit. I was thinking that his cousin Khalid is lucky that I was contacted instead of an actual hit man. Things might have unfolded differently for him. He might have ended up in the morgue with a toe tag that read Khalid Azizi.

Once outside in the parking lot, the warm breeze was a clear reminder of the beauty of freedom. Prison was a hell-hole. The steel gate had closed behind me with loud thud. I was glad I was going home, but as for Wal, he'll most likely spend the next 10 to 20-years of his life in prison. I'm anxious to talk to Khalid. I hoped he'd be another source of information for me on the street.

Chapter Twenty-Five

Denise heard the door open and yelled out from the kitchen, "Hey you."
I smelled the aroma of something wonderful cooking. "Hey, what smells so good?"
"I'm roasting chicken and potatoes." Denise loves to cook. Last summer, Denise had taken a cooking class at the Ripert Culinary School in Manhattan.

She hurried out of the kitchen. She looked seductive, even with an apron on. She flung the dishrag over her shoulder as she gave me a huge hug. "How was your day?"

"Better now that I'm home with you," I remarked.
"Fantastic," she said and walked back into the kitchen. The aroma was killing me, making my mouth water. "Damn, Denise, the chicken smells good."

"It's my Aunt Margret's recipe. Chicken with herbs and sherry wine."
Oh my God, I thought, if we didn't have all this shit going on in our lives, life could be so amazing.

Denise appreciated that John and Pete were so accommodating. On her way home from work, she asked them to stop at the liquor store so she could pick up a bottle of white wine to go with the dinner she was making tonight. What they didn't tell her, but told me later, was that the black Lincoln that had been following me had passed them as Pete doubled parked in front of Johnson's Liquor store. They said that they didn't want to pursue the Lincoln because Denise was in the car. After walking Denise to our apartment they waited for a bit to see if the Lincoln showed up. They saw me walk into the building then they broke off surveillance after an hour.

We ate, trying to keep the conversation light, but in the back of our minds, the things going on in both our lives were keeping us stressed. I remember getting into bed early that night, concerned about what our future might hold.

Chapter Twenty-Six

In the morning, I filled in Captain C.J. Matthews on my visit with Wal Azizi. C.J. has a reputation in the department as a detail oriented man. He has no tolerance for sloppy work. He agreed that the next step for me was to have a heart to heart talk with Khalid Azizi. C.J. asked that I bang out a report for distribution. I'm sure that Beau Winslow will want to get the case to the Grand Jury as soon as possible, before a preliminary hearing is scheduled and Wal finds out that he was dealing with an undercover cop. C.J. mentioned that the analysis on the laptop and cell phone seized at Carroll Street had been completed. One name kept popping up, Mustafa Salib. He mentioned that Salib was alleged to be behind the Carroll Street virtual kidnapping con. Salib is an illegal from Syria who's on the Terrorist Watch List. Evidence seized, led us to to an Arabic deli in the Soundview section of the Bronx. The FBI Terrorist Task Force has been notified, given the information, with any luck they may be able to come up with Salib's location.

I asked Joe and Angel if they would be available to come along later this evening, to pay Khalid Azizi a visit at his apartment. Joe replied, "Hell yes!" I could hear Angel in the background say, "Whatever Frankie needs."

C.J. walked over to my desk with a concerned look on his face. I asked, "Anything wrong Cap?"

He said, "It's Detective Carl Frazier. He's been screwing one of the secretaries in the office. His girlfriend called his house last night, unfortunately for him, his wife picked up the phone."

"Oh no," I said, trying to hide the slight grin. "Shit Cap, I'm not judging the guy but it was bound to happen. If they can walk and talk, Carl tries to get-em in the sack."

C.J.'s face was red from the constant aggravation he has to deal with. "Um yeah," he said, "Our administrative secretary, Tiffany Roper called Frazier's house last night. She spoke to Carl's wife, Tina. Tiffany told Tina that Carl has been sleeping with her for months and promised her a future with him."

"Shit," I said, in disbelief, "the guy must have a death wish."

Carl, in his early thirties, is a good looking guy, who can't keep it in his pants. He was fast asleep when the home phone rang. Tiffany told his wife and I'm paraphrasing, "My name is Tiffany Roper, I work with Carl. I want to let you know that your husband has been fucking me for six months and promised me that he was going to leave you." Tiffany hung up. Now, Carl's wife wants a divorce. The squad has had its share of sticky situations, now Frazier joins the roster.

The morning was flying by. Chief Larry Christopher called a meeting with me, Beau Winslow and C.J. Matthews in his office.

"Guys pull up a chair," the chief said. The chief, a chain smoker, lit cigarettes end to end during the meeting. He said in a friendly Bronx brogue, "Good job with Azizi, Frank. I need to inform the DA." He took a deep drag on his cigarette. "I understand," he continued, "Wal Azizi wants you to take his cousin out because he screwed him on a drug deal. Is that right?"

I couldn't help but notice that the chief looked like crap. He appeared drowsy and his skin was flushed. Maybe he's coming down with something. Come to think of it, he hasn't been his old self since the skiing accident he had in Aspen last year. It left him with chronic back pain that only pain-killers relieved. He sang the drugs praises at the time, calling them a wonder drug that allowed him to heal. But that was then, this is now.

"That's about the size of it chief," I shrugged, all the while thinking about him coming on to Tyra. Thoughts of Larry groping Tyra made my skin crawl. Maybe it's best rather than confronting Larry about it, that Tyra speak directly to C.J. Matthews about her sensitive dilemma.

I glanced at Beau and C.J. and said, "The game plan is to have a chat with Khalid tonight. Nulligan and Angel are gonna join me."

The chief leaned forward in his chair, looking a bit uneasy and said, "Damn Frank, be extra careful. Understand?"

Chief Christopher grabbed another cigarette and this time lit a match to it. He drew on it so intensely that he burned his fingers with the match. "Ouch, son of a bitch," Christopher yelled.

"Careful Chief," Beau said. "You okay Larry?"

Larry looked dazed. "Now where were we? Help me out here."
"We were just ending the meeting chief," C.J. said.

"Er...okay, meeting adjourned," Larry mumbled

"Okay then, Frank," C.J. said, "see what Khalid has to say and what he wants to do. I don't have to tell ya, if you see any contraband in his apartment, lock his ass up."

Chapter Twenty-Seven

Joe's C.I. has a new guy to score cocaine from. Two days ago, when Joe's confidential informant (C.I.) was making a buy, he got a glimpse of what appeared to be bomb making material in one of the back rooms in the drug dealers apartment. The dealer took note and quickly closed the door. Their conversation turned back to the coke deal. Luckily in one of our frequent conversations, Joe had told his informant Jack to keep his antennae up for anything related to bomb making. Bingo! Ali Elsayed.

It was hard for me not to get excited about the C.I.'s information. This is the first good lead we've had about a person who might be making bombs.

"Frankie, we're gonna bust this guy and squeeze him. Maybe he knows something about who tried to kill you," Joe said.

We all understood the implications and the importance of getting to Elsayed as fast as we could. My mind was running wild. Maybe he was the one who planted *my* bomb. I wanted to question him and make him talk. However, because of this new lead, Khalid Azizi would have to remain on the back burner.

It's amazing how plans can change on a dime. It's true, nothing ever stays the same. Last year Joe had locked up Jack for selling him an ounce of heroin; charging him with sale of a controlled substance, a B felony. Joe made him an offer he couldn't refuse, work for Joe as a C.I. or *do not pass Go and go directly to jail*. Jack accepted Joe's gracious offer and avoided jail.

Jack Bolster, a stone coke head, had scored an eight ball (1/8 ounce) of coke from the towel head, Ali Elsayed. Now we've got Elsayed by his short hairs. We're gonna pay Ali a visit tonight, but first we need a search warrant in hand to go along with our visit. "We'll send the informant in to make another buy before we hit the place." Joe chuckled and said, "With two buys under our belt, we'll have this prick by his balls."

Angel made a suggestion about searching Elsayed's apartment and his subsequent arrest. "Uh by the way Frankie, why don't you give Sal and your brother a call? I'm sure they'd be very interested in Elsayed, especially if he's making bombs."
"Good idea Angel," I said. "We need to touch base with Kip Patel in Intelligence. He has to find out all he can on this mope before we take his door down."

Although Azizi is on the sidelines for now, he's still at the forefront of my mind. I couldn't wait to hear what he had to say, who knows, maybe he's heard of Ali Elsayed.

I called Kip, the detective sergeant in charge of our intelligence squad. I gave him everything we had on Ali Elsayed. Beau prepared the search warrant for Elsayed's apartment. No question about it, we were all on an adrenaline high. Angel and Tyra went to their lockers to gear up for tonight's caper. Tyra strutted confidently out of the locker room casually dressed. Heads turned, eyeing her lustfully as she returned to her desk. I couldn't help but notice that Joe couldn't disguise just how sexy he thought she was. He was almost slobbering.

The affidavit to search Elsayed's apartment at Eastchester Road, Bronx, NY was written and had to be signed by a judge. Joe and Beau brought it to County Court Judge Frank Quantum. The judge signed the warrant and with that in hand, we were ready to rock and roll.

Detective Patel called. He'd completed the background investigation on Elsayed. I scribbled down the information. I mumbled to myself as I took notes. "US Immigration Service..... FBI's terrorist watch list......he's Syrian born..... here on a work visa..... he is twenty four..... lives in apartment 5J, fifth floor…..the utilities are in his name….. 5'8''….. 180 pounds….. black hair….. brown eyes….. owns a 2002 blue Toyota Camry, NY registration # BXY 645, listed at his Pelham address…… US Immigration Service queried….. visa issued on August 2, 2003….. reason for visiting the US….. work-related…. occupation….. engineer."

As soon as I put the receiver down, I held up the notepaper, waving it over my head and said, "The guy's here on a visa." I began to reiterate what Kip had found out. "We gotta be careful when we make the arrest; he's on the terrorist watch list." The thought of locking this guy up and questioning him made the hair on the back of my neck tingle. He may hold the key to who wants me out of the way and why. He may even have made the bomb that nearly killed me.

I got a text from Mike. "Doing okay?"

"Doing great," I replied. "Just got a hot lead on a bomb maker, gotta run."

"Careful, buddy," he texted back.

Operation Ali commenced. Tyra and I jumped into the Vette. Our caravan cautiously circled the target premises. Good news. Ali's car was parked in front and all four apartments on the fifth floor were lit up. We proceeded to rendezvous with Ace, Rich and more crucially, Jack Aloysius Bolster, C.I.

Most people imagine undercover operations to be carried out by a scruffy looking character wearing a hidden wire taped to his chest in order to capture some incriminating audio. Movies and TV shows have shown the bad guys patting down disguised cops and associates for signs of the dreaded tell-tale wire. Our office is equipped with state of the art eavesdropping technology. We have law enforcement specific software "The Ghost" used in conjunction with an iPhone app and a tiny device that can be strategically worn. The end results are nothing short of spectacular audio and video. Kudos to "Body Wire" technology.

Truthfully, we were all getting a bit nervous. We had a lot riding on Bolster. We wondered what was keeping him. If he didn't show up, the night was a bust. Joe was seething. He threw his hands in the air and yelled, "It's seven forty-five, where is the motherfucker?" Saliva was shooting from his mouth. Some of it hit my face as he continued his profanity laced tirade. Joe looked down the street and saw Jack slowly approaching. The misfit looked like he didn't have a fucking care in the world. Joe's face was etched in anger; he could hardly speak. "Okay, here he comes, that lazy ass fuck."

Jack strolled up to us nonchalantly like he was going to a Yankee game. Joe's jaw tightened in anger. His Irish temper boiling over, Joe lunged at the pathetic bastard, digging his fingers into Jack's throat and pushing him backwards onto the Vette. The ulcerated junky squealed like a pig and turned a shade of blue, trying to loosen Joe's grip. Ace grabbed Joe's fingers, finally prying them off Jack's throat. Joe started for Jack again but Rich and Tyra stepped in front of Joe, pushing him back. "Joe that's enough," Richie yelled. Joe was out of control. Jack was bent over, his hands rubbing his throat and gasping for in air. Joe had stepped away trying to compose himself. Jack stuttered as he spoke. "Sorry...Sorry Joe...I'm sorry, the time got away from me." Jack leaned back on the Vette as Joe glared at him for a moment and said, "Sorry, I'll give you sorry, you little douche bag. Next time, be on time!"

We all saw how upset Jack was. Richie diffused the situation by dragging Jack into Joe's car. He tried to relax the terrified waif so Jack could give a convincing performance in 5J.

Nervous energy soaring, the team donned our protective vests and raid jackets with "Police" emblazoned on them. The slides of the semi automatic pistols were racked. We were ready for war. By now, Jack was ready to get his dog and pony show on the road. Richie outfitted our man Bolster with a baseball cap housing the concealed transmitter.

We knew that Bolster was a flimsy decoy but he was all we had. He was motivated to cooperate. " Jack, don't do all the talking. Let Ali incriminate himself. We need him recorded. Got it?" I said. Jack nodded in agreement.

By now Joe had calmed down enough and said in a rough tone, "Dip-shit, find out what else he might be up to, then make the buy and get out." Joe dug down into his pocket, fished out three, one hundred dollar bills, counted it, held up three fingers, pushing his hand toward Jack's face and said, "Here's three hundred. Do your thing."

Jack grabbed the money and shoved it into the pocket of his grey jacket. His head was down. He didn't make eye contact with Joe. Jack, bearly able to speak said, "Be right back."
"Go and remember, come directly back to the car. Ya understand me?" Joe barked.

Rubbing his throat, again, Jack replied, "Yeah Joe, I understand."

Bolster started down the street toward the building. We jumped into Joe's car. Angel turned on the adapter to monitor Jack's conversation. Jack made his way to the multifamily house; we could hear his foot steps as he approached the building. Jack stopped and said, "I'm right in front. The lights are on in his apartment. Joe, I hope you can hear me. I'm walking in now." For a short time there was nothing being transmitted. The next thing we heard was a loud knock on a door, a split second later, a blood curdling scream. "Ahhhhhhhh, no!" We didn't know what to think. Seconds later, we heard Jack cry out, "Uh, oh my God! Oh my God, it's awful! All the fucking blood! He's fucking dead! Ali's dead!"

Jack high-tailed it out of the apartment like the rabid dog was chasing him. We threw the cars into drive and headed toward the building. It looked like Jack's feet didn't hit he ground as he ran towards us.

We met him in the middle of the block. Heaving for air, Jack muttered, "He's....he's.... dead...... the guy's dead!" Jack was shaking so intensely that I thought he'd pass out. Neighbors rushed out of their houses to see what the commotion was all about. Jack managed to get enough air into his lungs and grunted, "Joe, Joe, you gotta see this! His head! His fucking head is lying on the dining room table! Oh my God!"

We froze not fully getting the impact of what he had just said. I can't speak for the rest of the crew but a chill ran down my spine. I dreaded the thought of what I was about to see. Minutes later we burst through the front door and up the stairs to Ali's apartment. What we saw was fucking brutal. My eyes glanced around the apartment, coming to rest on Ali's head, propped up on the dining room table. His mouth and eyes were wide open. His face was frozen in fear. There was blood everywhere. It slowly dripped to the floor, pooling around the table leg. This is what hell must look like. If hell doesn't look like this, it's a close second. Our shoes became completely soaked in blood as we walked around the crime scene. The fucking place had been ransacked. Besides some cheap furniture, there wasn't much else in the joint. Lying on the living room floor was the rest of Ali's body. Blood was still oozing from the trunk of his neck where his head once sat. The killer left his calling card, the machete used to decapitate Ali was on the table.

We stood over his lifeless body. This is what radical Islam is all about. They're out to inflict terror. Angel, a tough cop, was in the bathroom, throwing up his guts. We were all sickened and numb.

Some shrinks recommend exercise as one of the ways to relieve stress. A jog across the Mohave Desert couldn't ease the tension we all encountered at this horrific scene. I'll get my workout with Makers Mark 90% Bourbon alone in the dark; some things can never be unseen. The brain has a limited focus and one can only keep so many images in its immediate sphere of awareness. Trying to replace the image of Ali's head, set on the table in that abysmal apartment, would be like trying to erase the Rosetta Stone. Impossible!

Law enforcement professionals infamously deal with stress by having affairs, too much booze or the ultimate finality, eating the gun. All of us in this apartment today are subject to those possibilities. We are very strong individuals but under certain circumstances anyone can crack.

Ace turned to me, rubbing his chin, shaking his head in disbelief and said, "Cheech, you'd better call the M.E.'s office."

The room reeked of congealing blood. Joe looked over at Angel who was wiping the vomit from his lips and said, "Hey Angel, you okay?"

Angel cleared his throat and said in a muffled voice, "Does it look like I'm fucking okay?"

He knew we understood, as we looked at Ali's decapitated corpse. My brother growled, "Christ, how could anybody do this?"

It seemed like an eternity, standing there trying to make sense of it all but of course we couldn't. Tyra felt woozy and quickly sat on a folding chair. My brother dashed to an open window for some fresh air. Ultimately, we began our search and I discovered a small amount of white powdery substance on the floor of the closet. Forensics later proved it to be ammonium nitrite, a highly explosive component of bomb making.

We notified the NYPD and the ME's office. Ace and I looked for anything that might have been left behind. In short order, Angel pulled himself together and began to look around the kitchen.

It wasn't long before Tyra and my brother resurfaced from the bedroom. Richie held up two pictures. They were photos of me and Denise leaving our apartment building. I ripped them out of his hand, staring at them so hard I could have burned a hole through them. "Frankie," Richie said, "Tyra found them behind the dresser. Whoever went through the apartment didn't know they were there."

We found the bomb maker, but someone got to him before we did. Someone silenced him before he could be questioned, but of the most concern were the photos.

We waited for the local cops and the guys from the M.E.'s office to wrap things up before we left. As far as Jack Bolster went, I guess what he saw blew his mind and he's still running. At some point, Joe will catch up with him and get the $300 and the hat back.

The press began calling the office and hounding Hogan for information about the murder of Elsayed. Word leaked out that Elsayed was beheaded and bomb making material was found in his apartment. No sooner than we returned to the squad room, Beau walked in. "John Xavier wants a meeting ASAP to discuss Ali Elsayed. I'll see you all there."

When everyone was in place, Hogan stood up behind his mahogany desk. "I know you're tired and in need of rest. I'm happy that you're all here in one piece. I know things got a bit hairy tonight. I understand that photos of Frank and Denise were found in the apartment. Several areas of concern need to be addressed before you leave. Most pressing is the threat to Frank's and Denise's lives. Captain Matthews, I want eyes on Frank and Denise 24/7 till I direct otherwise. Secondly, we need to utilize all our resources in the investigation of the murder of Elsayed. NYPD and our office will work in conjunction on the homicide."

"With all due respect Mr. Hogan, I'd rather deal with this situation by myself. I don't need a bodyguard."

"I'm gonna have to disagree Frank. I have a moral obligation to you and Denise," Hogan said. "The pictures of you and Denise send a very ominous message, we need to be diligent. These people are relentless."

Chief Christopher walked in late. Hogan was understandably perturbed. "Why are you late Larry?" Hogan said. "This meeting is very important!"

Larry looked like shit. A hangover? He was tongue tied and didn't reply. He simply took a seat.

Tyra and Joe shared a glance, as if to say, *looks like Larry's bombed again.*

Hogan continued, "We need to talk to our informants. These people have to be stopped. We need to shake up our informants till something falls out of the tree."

Hogan looked at each one of us and said, "I think we're done here. You know my feelings. I've got a press conference in twenty minutes. Chief Christopher, please keep me informed."

Chapter Twenty-Eight

Sleepless in New York. That was me. Images of Ali's head danced around in my thoughts like a jitterbug. "The Power of Now" wasn't working for me. Coming face to face with pure evil kept my eyes wide open. My restlessness awakened Denise. "Baby you okay? Can't sleep?"

"No, not tonight. Sleep won't come easy tonight. There was a gruesome crime scene on the job. I just can't un-see it. A guy was decapitated."

Denise sat up and fumbled to turn the night-lamp on. She didn't look at me and stared straight ahead. "Did you see it happen, Frank?"

"No, but the aftermath was the worst thing I've ever seen in my life."

Denise said tenderly, "I'm so sorry that you have to go through something so horrible. Can you tell me more about it? What happened?"

"I will, but not now. It feels good just to have you near me. Try to go back to sleep. I can't lie here and fester anymore."

I staggered into the kitchen, turned on the radio and made some coffee. The news report covered Elsayed's murder. I shut it off quickly so Denise didn't hear it. I waited for sunrise and then quietly dressed. The protection detail soon arrived. Pete and John were dressed to the nines; these seasoned detectives took special pride in their appearance. Starched white shirts, silk ties and Italian tailored suits. They had panache. They took their usual seats on the couch as I brought them coffee. I heard Denise stirring in the bedroom. She was sitting on the end of the bed reading her Facebook messages when I walked in. "Hey," I said forcing a smile, "Pete and John are here." I stood over her and began to gently massage her shoulders and said, "I'm gonna head out."

She looked up, her lips drawn tight and said, "Did you get any rest?"

"Not really, but I'm okay," I said gently stroking her hair, bending down to kiss her lips softly.

I filled my travel mug with black coffee and headed to my car. I noticed the familiar black Lincoln up the street. I decided to pull out and see what happens. It followed me at a safe distance. I tried to see who was driving but the tinted windows made that difficult. I made some hasty maneuvers to see if it was gonna continue to follow me. It did. My tail mimicked my every move. I pulled out my 9 mm and placed on the seat next to me. The thought crossed my mind to try and stop the car myself, but I came up with a better plan. I radioed the dispatcher in the office. I reported the tail and gave instructions for Nulligan and a team of detectives to position themselves on the off ramp, at exit 6, on I-287 East. I was hitting speeds of 80 mph on the curvy Bronx River Parkway, breaking almost every traffic law in the book.

I exited the Parkway at the County Center, blew the traffic light on Route 119. It was about a half mile to I-287 and the sons of bitches were right behind me. I radioed dispatch. The blockade was in place. I sped onto the expressway. The Lincoln followed suit and was now about five cars behind me. The exit ramp was just one mile up ahead. I exited the interstate and onto the ramp at a high rate of speed. Unmarked police cars were blocking the ramp. Detective George Way, a detective in his mid-fifties, with an aggressive attitude stood with Angel bracing themselves behind their cars, with guns drawn. I sped up along side them, screeching to a stop. The Lincoln, was so far up my ass, it had no where to go, sliding to a stop in front of George and Angel. The occupants of the Lincoln were now looking down the barrels of guns.

Pistol in hand, I jumped out of my car. My heart was pounding and the adrenaline rushed through me like shit through a goose. By the time I got to the Lincoln, George and Angel had two guys out of the car and face down on the pavement in handcuffs. They were screaming at the top of their lungs, "FBI, we're FBI agents! We can explain!" I stood over them yelling, "Explain, explain, why the fuck have you been following me?"

The taller one tried to get up, but I stomped my foot between his shoulder blades, forcing him back on his stomach. He grimaced in pain yelling, "Hey, my credentials are in the inside pocket of my suit jacket. I'm Special Agent Ken Spencer. We have specific orders not to let you out of our sight this week. There is a heavy threat on your life."

His partner, who was also face down on the ground was grumbling, "We have credible information that you are in imminent danger."
Angel and George grabbed the handcuffs and yanked them to their feet, forcing them back against the Lincoln. They were agitated to say the least, attempting to move away from the car. Angel shoved them back against the car. George removed their credentials from their suit jacket to verify their identity. Their FBI badges were clearly visible in a small leather holder fastened to their belts. "Why didn't you just let Frank know that you were keeping an eye on him?" Angel yelled. "You could have been hurt."
Nulligan's flashing emergency lights and siren were blaring. He came to a halt, burning rubber and ran over to the cluster fuck of cops and agents. Joe's Irish was up. He was almost nose to nose with the agents. "They're FBI agents," George yelled.

Joe curled his hands into a fist and raised them at the agents. "Whoa, agents?" he shouted, looking back at us.

"Yeah, we're FBI," Agent Spencer huffed. Spencer is a strapping guy, in his early forties, with riveting blue eyes. He was clearly shaken and embarrassed. He barked, "Look, we had our orders. Now take the fuckin' cuffs off!"

The traffic at the exit was backed up for a half mile. We had to cut these guys loose. We had no choice. Angel turned them around, un-cuffing them. They now had to give the bad news to their superiors that they were stopped in a road block, set up by detectives from the DA's office. The curiosity was killing me. Pushing past the detectives and up to the agents, I said, "I'm not gonna ask ya twice, are you the two birds that met with Mike Baraka in front of his building the other day?" Stunned for a moment, they dropped their heads and didn't respond. Finally Agent Spencer lifted his head, looked me square in the eye and shook his head yes. He then clumsily said, "Yes, it was us."

"So you've been pressuring Baraka to keep tabs on his cousin Hani when he's released from prison," I said.
They shook their heads yes. The agents got into their cars and police vehicles were pulled off the ramp to let the traffic by. As the agents pulled past us, Spencer picked up the mic on the two way radio and mouthed something into it. The expression on his face said it all. He wasn't happy. I guess he was giving the dispatcher the awkward news.

We returned to the office and debriefed Captain Matthews. Matthews said, "The FBI agents should have handled this differently. This office should have been in the loop. All of this drama could have been avoided. Now, speaking of drama, we must get to the bottom of why Elsayed was murdered. It's not like a scorned lover came in and stabbed him with a nail file. This was a vicious beheading reeking from the stench of terrorism."

Chapter Twenty-Nine

Mike sounded edgy when he called. The first thing he spat out was, "Frank, I heard what happened in the Bronx. It's all over the news. The guy was butchered. How ya doin?"

"It was a fucking nightmare. Use your imagination."

"Uh, yeah, I'll bet it was. Sorry."

"Yeah, sorry," I said in a dour tone.

"Anyway, what's going on with you Mike?"

"Uh, well," he said, "I thought you should know that my cousin Ayman is out of prison. Uh, he paid me an unexpected visit early this morning."

I was all ears. I wanted to know exactly what his cousin was up to. I asked excitedly, "Oh, tell me everything. I want to know everything he said and most importantly where I can find him."

Mike was uneasy. "Frankie, he didn't say where he's staying. The fucking bastard tried to recruit me into his fucking radical Islamic bullshit. All his life he was Christian. Now he's a radical Muslim and wants to kill infidels, people like you."

"Look Mike", I said, "did he mention me specifically?"

"No, no he didn't."

"I want you to string him along," I said. "I wanna find out what his plans are." The phone went silent for a second. "Hey Mike, you there?"

"Yeah Frank, I'm here. I'll find out what I can," he said, sounding reluctant.

"Good," I said, pressing him. "Did he say anything else?"

Grudgingly, Mike replied, "He's recruiting others for a holy war and wants me to help him. I told him to leave me the fuck alone. I'm not interested in his fucking holy war."

I wanted to ask, why the hell didn't you find out where he living? Why didn't you ask? You know I'd want to know where he's staying. "Mike, we're at war with these people," I barked. "It's happening on American soil." I continued to admonish him. "Give the FBI a call. They need to know this too."

Mike launched into a tirade of four letter expletives. "Frank, I want to be fucking left alone. I'm only doing this for you. I don't want to get involved with the FBI!" "If you don't call, I'll call the fucking FBI! I think it's important that they have this information. Besides, they stopped by your house last week. I saw you talking to them."

"You saw them?"

"Yeah, I saw them."

"Frankie, they refuse to leave me alone."

Chapter Thirty

The four Musketeers, me, Joe, Tyra and Angel cautiously approached Khalid Azizi's Carpenter Avenue apartment building. We eye-balled his late model silver Oldsmobile Intrigue at the curb. Joe and Angel were winded as we made our way to the fourth floor level. We un-holstered our weapons and took positions on either side of the door, as Joe forcefully banged on the door of apartment 4B. No response. He pounded it again, this time warning, "Police, open up." The door opened slightly. Khalid yelled, "What do you want? I haven't done anything!" Tyra barked, "Just remove the chain and let us in, we need to ask you a few questions." Reluctantly, Khalid obliged. Angel barreled into the apartment and shoved Khalid down in a chair.

"What do you want? I told the cops everything. I have nothing more to say about Wal."

Khalid was sweating bullets and fidgeting frantically. "Please, what do you want from me? How do I know you're cops, show me some I.D."

Joe took his badge from under his shirt and planted it squarely in Khalid's face.

"Ok. Ok," he replied.

Joe said gruffly, "Let's get right down to the nitty-gritty. Your wacked out cousin, Wal, hired Frankie, right here, to kill your sorry ass; to put a gun to your head and pull the trigger. Luckily for you, it was Frankie instead of a real hit man."

"That fuck," Khalid mumbled.

"Yeah," I said, "that fuck paid me to take you out. With you gone, he was back on the street."

Tyra and Angel began the search of Khalid's apartment, while I nosed around the bedroom, with Khalid in tow. There was a photo of Khalid in a desert setting, dressed in an Arab tunic and headpiece, holding what looked like a Russian AK47 rifle. He looked like he was ready for battle. There were a bunch of papers sitting on the dresser. I began to thumb through them. There was an unpaid phone bill, electric bill and a letter post marked from Syria. I tore open the letter. It was written in Arabic, I slid the letter back into the envelope.

Joe called dispatch and requested the canine unit. Detective Freddy Hopper arrived with Eureka. Eureka is Freddy's star German shepherd methodically trained to sniff out drugs wherever they're hidden. Hopper is the most highly recognized New York specialist in his field. Khalid's face dropped as Eureka headed swiftly into the bedroom. The dog alerted aggressively as she approached the closet. Eureka pawed and dug at the exact spot where she detected the smell of narcotics under some lose floorboards. Dogs like Eureka have been instrumental in assisting law enforcement in their quest to halt drug trafficking since the early 1970's. They have become an invaluable resource in the war on drugs.

Angel removed some boxes from the closet. Eureka was pawing the closet floor with fervor. Angel removed the floorboards there were several bricks of what appeared to be narcotics. A quick field test, proved them positive for heroin. Game over.

"That's not mine! I don't know how it got there!" Khalid cried. He was handcuffed and I had the pleasure of reading him his Miranda Rights. Angel and Tyra escorted him to a waiting police car.

Khalid was in the interrogation room waiting for his questioning to begin. All of our interrogations are audio and video recorded. Matthews, Beau and I decided to use an accusatory approach to his interrogation. I have found that in cases like this one, at first, a form of monologue is better than Q & A format. My demeanor will be patient, understanding and non-degrading. My objective is to make Khalid gradually more comfortable with telling the truth. Of course there will be an implicit assumption of his guilt in my technique. Beau insisted that I read him his Miranda Rights again. I began, "Khalid, we have concrete evidence against you for possession of heroin. There's no escaping it. Maybe Wal was a big influence on your decision to traffic in heroin. If Wal coerced you, tell us now. He's a bad apple. Maybe he threatened you and your family. We want to help you here, but you gotta come clean. We need to put Wal away permanently. You are here on an expired visa. You can help. Your cooperation will work for you, down the road, we'll see to that."

"You can't stop Wal, as long as he's alive." Khalid uttered, as he made eye contact with each of us. "I'm scared shitless of him. If he finds out I'm talking....I want a lawyer." His agitation grew as he wrestled with the handcuffs.

Matthews interrupted, "Ok. Have it your way, but know that your best shot at leniency is to cooperate now."

"I'll discuss it with my lawyer," Khalid replied sarcastically.
Khalid was transported to the County Jail, awaiting his arraignment.

Chapter Thirty-One

God, it's tough being Frank Santorsola. The earth continues to revolve around the sun, but I have no leads as to who specifically has a hit out on me. The last several days, have been the likes of which I've never experienced in my career. We are all feeling the fallout. We owe it to ourselves and each other to stay focused and be on top of our game.

Denise was concerned about my mental welfare and strongly encouraged me to meet with the department shrink. My only experience with a shrink was back in my early career. In order to gain entry to the police department, I had to meet with Dr. Karl Bachon. Dr. Bachon was devoid of any manner, bedside or other. He was rude and abrupt. He wore a forest green corduroy jacket with leather elbow patches; he curiously focused his questions on my sexual nature. I think he was a closet perv who got off on this line of questioning. My relationship with my mother, female and male cousins, childhood classmates etc, were at the forefront of the session. He straightened his polka-dotted bow tie every few minutes and never cracked the slightest smile. He was new to the position and I heard he didn't finish the first six months on the job. Good riddance, Dr. B! I really think he was the one who needed a good therapist. Since then, I'm reluctant to see another psychiatrist. I told Denise I'd like to give it some time before I made that decision. She agreed.

Mike insisted on meeting me for lunch, even though I told him I was up to my eyeballs in shit. As a courtesy, I agreed to meet him. We planned to meet at Vesna's Café in Tuckahoe. It's one of my favorite spots to stop in and get the best lunch in Westchester.

Vesna and Milovan Anic fled war-torn Mostar, Bosnia Herzegovina, in the early 1990's. While Vesna was in the hospital giving birth to their first born son, Mark, enemy troops invaded the city and seized the Anic's home. The young couple was never to enter their house again. Courageously, they grabbed their piece of the great American dream and have prospered here in New York.

"Ah, hello Franjo!" Vesna said. "What will you have today?"

"My mouth has been watering for some of your mushroom soup and ustipci," I replied.

Mike said he was starving and said, "Vesna, I'll have the same."

"Grandma Matija's mushroom soup, coming right up," said the gorgeous slender Croatian woman.

"So Mike, tell me what's up?" I asked.

Mike smiled and said excitedly, "Cindy and I are getting hitched. We both want you and Denise to come to our wedding."

I was dumbstruck. Startled by the fact that Cindy agreed to marry him and make him a permanent fixture in her life. Truthfully, I was surprised by his decision, as well.

"Mike, first of all, my sincere congratulations. Cindy is a fine woman. You're a lucky man," I said.

Mike, replied, "I can't have Santino grow up without his parents being married, now can I? It's the only way for me. Our relationship isn't perfect but the marriage is a must. We will work through whatever we need to. Santino comes first."

"So, will you come?" Mike asked.

"Mike, it's not that simple. You must know my office frowns on any type of personal interaction with anyone connected to criminal activities. Cindy's father is in the mob. You were a federal informant. I don't know? I can't say yes right now."

Our soup was served. It interrupted the awkward exchange. Mike looked dejected. "I don't understand," he continued, "Cindy has nothing to do with her fathers business."

"Mike, I'm happy for you and Cindy. I'm not sure I'll be there," I said.

"Maybe you'll come to the ceremony. It's Saturday. I'll text you the details."

Mike got up abruptly and left. I felt guilty, but not too guilty to continue enjoying the best mushroom soup on the planet.

Later that day, a suspicious metal canister was discovered in a trash bin by a passerby in the Theater District in New York City. A cell phone was attached to the can as a trigger mechanism. By 2:30 p.m., a large portion of Times Square was evacuated. This was a mammoth task and required all hands on deck. NYPD Bomb Squad was in the process of transporting the bomb, when we got the report of an explosion in the Meat Packing District in New York City. Twenty storefronts were destroyed and hundreds were injured, ten seriously. The bomb was hidden in the Sky Bridge connecting two buildings and tore through everything and everyone in its lethal path. ISIS claimed responsibility.

The Times Square bomb was taken to the police firearms range at Rodman's Neck in the Bronx. The Bomb Squad determined that the canister was a sarin bomb.

Since 9.11.01, we exist with the alarming knowledge that we are all targets of the madmen behind these incidents. They loathe our way of life and our Western Civilization. We are at war with these assholes. Innocent civilians are their soft targets.

Chapter Thirty-Two

I mulled over the idea of attending Mike's wedding. Still on the fence when I got up Saturday, I knew it was decision time. My curiosity got the better of me and I decided to go. There I was, 1:30 p.m., at Justice of the Peace Sy Sidney's house on Broadmoor Place in Yonkers. I sat in my car across the street to get a bird's eye view of the goings on. One by one a stream of family and friends entered the two story brick home. The beautiful bride arrived in a white stretch limo. She looked like one of the brides on "My Big Fat Gypsy Wedding." Cindy needed assistance from the bridesmaids to maneuver the large hoop-skirted dress out of the limo. She balanced an oversized, three tiered rhinestone tiara that hugged her bubble bun hair style planted squarely on top of her head. Anna Wintour, the editor of Vogue Magazine, would not approve. Cindy looked more like a bride at the Bellagio in Vegas, rather than one on Broadmoor Place. I guess she wasn't gonna let the venue dictate the way she dressed. Not one to be out done, Mike arrived separately. He wore a white brocade silk embroidered Sherwani, a long coat-like garment, with gold silk pants and matching gold silk slippers.

My next sighting was something out of the movie "Men in Black." At 1:45 p.m. a black Suburban SUV with tinted windows pulled up. Inside were three U.S. Marshals and Nick Galgano. Through the mercy of the court, Nick was granted permission to attend Cindy's wedding. In the wee hours of the morning, a contingent of U.S. Marshals escorted Nick from Allenwood Federal Prison in Pennsylvania to Yonkers. Three strapping Marshals exited the SUV and diligently looked around to make sure no threats were hiding anywhere on the mean streets of Yonkers, New York.

They wore simple black suits and sunglasses. One even had a black hat. All three wore earpieces for efficient communication. Next, a grim figure dominated the scene. Nicky *Blue Eyes* stood tall, looming over the others at 6 feet-four inches. The psychopath, hands in cuffs, looked like something out of a "B" movie. An ill fitting tuxedo was in stark contrast to his usual European tailored clothes. The men in black took Nick inside and over to his daughter. Cindy tried to hold back the tears. The site of her frail father plus the emotions of the day got the best of her. His recent heart surgery had left him looking old, tired, and nothing like the strong virile man he once was.

The ceremony room was filled with rows of white folding chairs. Splitting the room in half was a short aisle. It's seen its share of weddings, I assumed. I knew Nick was no threat, but I was on the look out for Mike's cousin Ayman Hani. He was a no show, I'm happy to say. It would have created a scene. Nick was seated in the front left row, flanked by two Marshals. The one wearing the black fedora stood guard at the entry.

Mike told me that Cindy agreed to partake in one of the beautiful customs his family cherished. The night before the wedding, the women gather together at a Mehendi ceremony held at the bride's house. They decorate her hands and feet with henna paste designs as they sing and tell stories. Mike's sister Delia is the most artistic of the group, so she did the work on Cindy. It was absolutely beautiful. It's the first time I'd ever seen such artwork.

I'm sure when Nick spotted it he was jolted. Pretty sure he's not familiar with it and he knows it's not an Italian thing. He'll have to just deal with it. He was lucky to be witnessing the wedding at all.

Judge Sidney took his place at the front of the room. Mike and his best man, his cousin Hussein, followed suit.

Scoliosis had gotten the better of Judge Sidney. He was slightly bent over and looked very uncomfortable. The 80 year old wore a black robe and held a bible in his arthritic hands. Mike swayed side to side from nerves. Hussein put his hand on Mike's back to steady him. Mikes eyes moved to his son Santino, sleeping angelically in the arms of his devoted Jaddah Adel. Nick was taken to the back of the room. Cindy grabbed his arm and they proceeded to walk down the aisle to the sweet tones of piped in music "Here Comes the Bride." Nick had to keep at a distance from the hooped dress so it didn't rise up. What a sight.

The father of the bride gave her away to her groom. He kissed his daughter gently on her cheek. They held their embrace for what felt like an hour. Their tears mixed together like Niagara Falls. Even I got choked up a little.

As Nick returned to his seat, our eyes locked. As they say, if looks could kill I'd be dead. The fuck blames me for ruining his life. He takes no blame upon himself for living the thug life for 35 years, literally getting away with murder throughout his nefarious career. The tension between us was palpable in the room. I think everyone could sense it.

The ceremony began, Mike and Cindy exchanged vows for better or for worse. I had the nagging feeling it was gonna be for worse. "You may now kiss the bride" was met with enthusiastic applause from the small crowd.

The entry foyer had a small table with several bottles of Veuve Clicquot and some plastic champagne flutes. The crowd gathered for a short toast. The Marshals took hold of Nick and walked him to the back of the room where he kissed his daughter and congratulated his son-in-law. He whispered something in Mike's ear. I saw the expression on Mike's face. It was one of mutual agreement. Adel rushed up with Santino. Nick smiled and kissed Santino on both cheeks, said something to Santino in Italian, but I couldn't hear what Nick said. I stayed out of his way. I didn't want to cause any bad vibes on Mike's happy day.

The Marshals were anxious to return Nick behind bars where he belonged. Cindy and Nick said their bittersweet farewells and off he went with his chaperones. I offered my best wishes to the newlyweds and made my exit.

"Wait Frankie, aren't you gonna come to the reception?" Mike asked. "Just stop by for a drink." he pleaded. "It's at Fayyad's, you know the place."

"Sorry Mike. I can't." Once again, he looked pierced by a sword.

Unbeknownst to Mike, I had plans to case the joint without making a big splash. I was good at this spy stuff. Fayyad's, which translated from Arabic to English means plentiful. It has a secluded back door to its second floor balcony. I snuck in and hid behind some storage crates while being extremely careful not to be detected. I arrived before the wedding guests so I could observe them entering the restaurant. After ten minutes they walked in. A three piece band began to play Arabic music. The wait staff served tabouleh, shanklish and kafta kebabs, among other Arabic delights.

The crowd was growing. Belly dancers gyrated to the rhythm of the music. Suddenly I spotted Ayman Hani. Even Mike looked surprised to see him, but welcomed him with open arms. Hani grabbed a drink and handed Mike an envelope, I imagine bursting with cash, a wedding gift? He made a quick departure. Remember, Hani is the very reason I didn't want to go to the reception. It would have been a calamity if we had bumped into each other. Doesn't Mike realize this? This was my first opportunity to tail Hani but by the time I got to my car, he had disappeared.

Chapter Thirty-Three

Another gorgeous sunrise in New York! I got a nice early start at the office arriving at 7 a.m. It's a rare occasion to have peace and quiet on the fourth floor on Martine Avenue and a great opportunity to get some important work done without any interruptions. At 7:30 a.m., I took a bathroom break. As I entered the men's room, I heard some whimpering sounds coming from one of the toilet stalls. I found Chief Larry Christopher in a fetal position on the floor of the second stall. The door was open, so I was able to get down on one knee to check his vitals. "Chief, what's wrong?" He grumbled and mumbled and finally came around. He was in some kind of altered state. Was he drunk or high? "I'm fine," he said. He managed to crawl his way up to a kneeling stance. His pupils were dilated and his eyes were blood shot.

"How did you end up here on the floor at 7:30 a.m.? Are you ok Chief? Should I call an ambulance?" I asked.

"Ambulance?" he slurred, "you never saw this, Santorsola. This never happened. Keep it to yourself. Understand?"

"Chief, I think you need some help. Can I call your wife?"

"When I want your opinion Santorsola, I'll give it to you."

I was between a rock and a very hard place. This was the chief ordering me to ignore a very problematic situation. What was protocol in a dilemma like this? I knew Larry was not himself lately but this behavior was off the charts. I helped him back to the privacy of his office and returned to the squad room. Well enough about getting some work done without interruption.

By now, people were populating the fourth floor at the usual pace. As soon as Captain Matthews arrived, he motioned me and Tyra to his office. Could he have heard about Larry somehow? If so, what would I say? "Frank, Tyra had the pictures she took on Carroll Street printed."

I had a temporary sigh of relief. "Oh yeah, the pictures," I said, "Let me see them."

Tyra handed me a collage of twenty photos. I scanned through them quickly and stopped short, about half way through. "What, Frankie, recognize someone?" Matthews chirped.

"Captain, I need to get my glasses. I'll take the pictures back to my desk. I'll report back."

"Ok. By the way," Matthew's said, "Chief Christopher called and cancelled all his meetings today. He's got the flu."

Yeah right, I thought. Good luck with that.

Back at my desk, I examined the photos more discreetly. I thought I saw someone I didn't want to see in those images. The first half was just a bunch of random people going in and out of the building, with a few junkies in the mix. A scrawny, strung out Liz Christopher appeared. Liz is the 23-year old daughter of Larry Christopher. She looked like the poster girl for Faces of Addicts.com. Liz was once pretty and a promising young piano prodigy. She dropped out of The Julliard School abruptly last year, now I know why. Boy, this is definitely a sad day for the Christopher's. Little Lizzie is a junkie. For the moment, I decided to keep this information to myself. She was a victim of the influx of illicit drugs streaming into the United States.

Joe walked in. I decided to tell Joe about Larry. "Joe, I've got something to tell you. It stays with us. It goes nowhere. Understand?"

I explained how I found Larry this morning. "That's why he called in sick this morning," Joe said.

"The flu, my ass," I scoffed. "What the fuck is going on with him? First he's coming on to Tyra. Now he's out of his mind, rolling around on the shit-house floor."

"Was he drunk?" Joe asked. "Are you gonna report him?"

"I don't think it was alcohol. Right now, I'm not sure what to do."

"Understood," Joe said.

Chapter Thirty-Four

The next morning Denise and I had a quick bite at Coffee Grinds in midtown Manhattan. Denise's ever vigilant bodyguards sat a few tables away from us. She took my hand and said, "How ya feeling hon?"

"Great, anytime I'm with you," I smiled.

We enjoyed each other for a bit and then went our separate ways. I watched her and the boys leave, singing to myself, *Through the Fire*, a song written by David Foster. One of my favorites. It's how Denise makes me feel. It's our song.

Off to the races. After a few meetings at the office, Joe and I decided to pick up a quick sandwich and return to the office to finish up some police reports. As we were walking across Martin Luther King Boulevard, I tripped on a crack and fell to one knee. Suddenly I heard a loud boom, like a cherry bomb. It was hard to distinguish which direction it came from. I heard a thud next to me. That was the sound of Joe landing on the pavement. In a flash, there was chaos all around us. A woman near us yelled, "The shot came from up there." She was pointing to the top of the nearby parking structure. I instinctively drew my 9 mm. My thoughts were racing. I grabbed Joe by the ankles and pulled him a few feet to safety. Now, we were behind a large circular planter and possibly out of harms way. I called to the woman, "Call 911, now!" Blood gushed from Joe's shoulder wound as I applied pressure, performing first aid to stem the bleeding. At the same time, I was focusing my attention to the top of the four story parking lot, looking for the shooter. Joe was heaving for air. His beige sports jacket was now half crimson. He was bleeding fast and profusely. I thought I was gonna lose him right then and there on the concrete. People were panicked, screaming and running for cover. One more shot rang out, but it missed its target. Instead it blew away part of a planter.

Tyra and a few other detectives ran out of the courthouse lobby and took cover, surrounding us for our protection. Good thing it was lunchtime, lots of the squad was just leaving the building. Sirens blaring, several reinforcements from the White Plains PD arrived, placing their sector cars in front of us, giving us additional cover. An ambulance crew soon arrived, put Joe on a gurney and transported him to the hospital. I was in a trauma induced fog but I rode with Joe and continued to talk to him all the way to the E.R.

The SWAT team had swarmed the parking structure. Equipped with M-14 assault rifles, shot guns, ballistic shields and body armor, they searched for the shooter. A clean sweep of the structure turned up several shell casings from a 7.62 round on the top level. No wonder there was a gaping hole in Joe, the size of a golf ball. No suspect was found but one of the witnesses thought the shooter might be a woman.

The ambulance pulled up to the sliding door entrance to the White Plains Hospital E.R. Luckily it was only a few blocks away from the courthouse. Joe was hooked up to a few I.V.'s and carefully wheeled into the triage unit. Joe was an ESI-Level 1(Emergency Severity Index.) The docs determined that immediate surgery was required to save his life. He was swiftly prepped and entered the operating room post-haste.

I needed to make some calls. I didn't want Jessica to hear it second hand, so I called her first. No answer. I left her a message to call me ASAP. Denise was next. She rushed to the hospital. The hospital waiting area was filling up with our comrades in arms. It was a sea of blue uniforms waiting vigil for their fellow brother to recover.
Jess called, "Hi Frank. Is everything okay? I've been trying to reach Joey."

"Jess, there was a shooting today. Joe was shot and he's in surgery right now. He's gonna be okay," I said trying to reassure her but I didn't know if he was going to make it.

"Is he okay? I mean really okay? Oh my God. Please say he's okay!" she cried.

"Listen Jess," I said, "stay where you are, I'll send a squad detective for you. He's in White Plains Hospital."

"I'm in Bloomingdales. I'll be there in a few minutes," Jess sobbed.

Captain Matthews and DA Hogan entered the waiting room. "Frank, what do you know about Joe's condition?" Hogan asked.

"One thing I know," I said, "Joe's lost a massive amount of blood. He hasn't regained consciousness since the bullet hit him. A nurse said it's touch and go. All we can do is pray and wait for the outcome of the surgery."
At breakneck speed Jessica ran over to us. "How is he? Where is he? What happened?" She cried and fell into my arms.

I held her close to me and said, "Jess, the doctors are doing everything they can."

I gave Hogan, Matthews and Jessica a brief synopsis of what went down outside the courthouse today. It's a tragedy but I'm grateful for the quick response from my fellow officers. The situation could have been much worse if not for them and their selfless actions.

Denise arrived with her security detail. She ran over to Jessica and whispered something in her ear. Jess hugged her as she wiped away her tears. I took Denise up to the cafeteria for coffee. It gave me the opportunity to fill her in . She softly wept while I gave her the gory details. She asked me why someone would want Joe dead. I thought to myself, maybe they wanted me dead, but hit Joe instead when I tripped on the walkway. I didn't let on to Denise; she had enough on her plate.

"We'll find the shooter," I said, "that's a promise."

We headed back down to the waiting room. John Hogan approached me and said, "Frank, meet me in my office at 4:00 p.m. I need to be debriefed on every inch of the shooting."

"Yes sir," I replied.

"By the way," Hogan said, "have you seen Larry Christopher today?"

"Not a trace," I replied bluntly.

Captain Matthews and I met in DA Hogan's at 4:00 p.m., on the dot. I'm a stickler for punctuality. Several recent studies suggest that type A and type B people actually feel time pass differently. For type A individuals, a minute passed in 58 seconds, where type B people felt a minute pass in a leisurely 77 seconds. That 18 second gap is considerable as time goes by. I guess I'm type A. I carefully relived the afternoon, moment by moment to the DA. Naturally Hogan was very alarmed by all the crazy stuff that's been going on lately. He has to handle the press.

"Mr. Hogan, I was thinking that maybe I was the intended target and Joe took a bullet meant for me."

"At this point, Frankie, anything is possible. You know we have you covered 24/7. That's part of the reason why the PD responded so quickly," Hogan said.

"Thanks, Mr. Hogan," I replied. "I can sleep a little better, knowing they're around."

I got back to the hospital by 6:00 p.m. After waiting for what seemed like an eternity, Dr. Zoya Viswanathan joined us in the waiting room. She looked way too young to be a surgeon. Dr. Viswanathan addressed the group. "I assume you're here for Mr. Nulligan?"

Jessica and her sister Carol were arm in arm waiting for the word about Joe. "Yes we are!" Jessica and Carol cried.

"Please step out into the hallway," the doctor said.

Jess, Carol and I followed her out.

"Mr. Nulligan has suffered a traumatic brachial plexus injury," the doctor said. As she was about to continue, Jessica interrupted her. "Is he going be okay?" she yelped.

"He will live," Dr. Viswanathan said. "The axons, which you can think of as copper filaments in an electric cable, have been severed. The prognosis is hard to predict. It varies from injury to injury. Only time will tell if he will regain full range of motion of his shoulder, arm or hand. Some patients have a spontaneous recovery following surgery, while others can take up to a year or perhaps not regain usage at all. I'm sorry, that is the best news I have for you."

"Can I see him now?" Jessica yelled.

"Sorry, but no," the doctor said, "he needs to be completely rested and sedated until morning. I suggest you all go home. He's fine for now."

Jessica, Carol and I were back at the hospital at 7 a.m. the next morning. Room 333 was filled with floral arrangements, cards and happy face balloons, wishing Joe a speedy recovery. Joe was groggy, but comforted that we were there. He didn't speak much and kept falling asleep. The truth is we were just happy to lay our eyes on him. Jessica and Carol were each holding one of his hands.

"Joey, I'll be back soon," I said cheerfully. "Rest, buddy. I gotta start looking for the prick that did this to you."

Joe raised his left thumb in a show of camaraderie. I left him there in the good care of Jessica, Carol and two White Plains PD officers posted at his door.

As I left the hospital, I was about to cross Chester Avenue, to the parking garage, when a car sped by me. I got a glimpse of the driver. It looked like Ayman Hani! Why would Hani be driving around White Plains at 8:00 a.m.? Was he returning to the scene of the crime, or maybe looking for me?

Chapter Thirty-Five

NoMAD- Manhattan---Even though the term was coined in 1990's for the neighborhood north of Madison Square Park, it really hasn't caught on yet. Now, however it has gained some undesired notoriety. NYPD confirms that a bomb containing the materials needed to make sarin was discovered in a trash bin in Madison Square Park. "NoMAD Bomb Trashed" was the headline of the NYC newspapers. Once again, a catastrophe was avoided due to the "see something, say something" mentality that has been etched into our psyche. Crisis averted for now.

Captain Matthews ordered in lunch for the two of us. He told me that the letter we found in Khalid's apartment was translated. The letter originally contained a key that Khalid was to use every Friday to open a luggage locker at Ionel's Juice Bar in Brighton Beach. In New York, a series of privately owned businesses like the juice bar will store luggage for a daily fee. A new startup company has taken an Airbnb style approach to luggage storage in Manhattan. It's a novel concept that is quite successful.

"Now," Matthews continued, "we need to contact the Westchester County Jail and hope they have a key in Khalid's personal effects. The letter directed Khalid to take the money in the envelope and get it to a person called Sayf, translated means blade or sword."

"Okay, Cap. I'll head over to the jail now," I replied. "Thanks for lunch."

I met with the property clerk at the jail and unfortunately, no key was found in Khalid's belongings. As I left the room, alarms sounded from a loud automated system, announcing that the jail was in lockdown mode. The ear-piercing volume was intentional to get everyone's attention. I remained near the property room until an all clear was broadcast, about one hour later. The suspense was killing me. The property clerk had left his post and ran after me. "Detective Santorsola," he shouted. "Looks like your guy got the sharp end of a shank in his chest. He was in the shower room. Somebody shanked him good."

"Khalid?" I said in shock. "Is he dead?"

"Yep."

I'm thinking, looks like our hunt for the Sayf just hit a brick wall.

Chapter Thirty-Six

The White Plains PD arrested an Asian guy on possession of cocaine. Phuc Nguyen doesn't want to spend anytime in the slammer; he has some credible information to trade. He claims to know someone who is selling black market explosives and cocaine.

Captain Matthews said, "Frankie, John Hogan is willing to barter this information and let Phuc Nguyen skate if he's proven reliable. Phuc is a predicate felon and will turn in his own mother to avoid the stiff jail sentence he will face."

"Let the games begin," I laughed. "When can I get to meet him?"

"Call Detective Willy Martinez, he will arrange the meeting. Phuc is out on bail. Good luck Frankie."

"Thanks, Captain."

Nguyen was a short order cook at Saigon Shack in Nyack, New York. His family evacuated Vietnam during the fall of Saigon in 1975 and landed in the United States. They were one of the lucky ones to escape the atrocities committed by the North Vietnamese, under the communist leader Ho Chi Minh. Many South Vietnamese people who cooperated with the American's were tortured and killed. Although several generations of Nguyen's family prospered in the states, Phuc did not follow suit. He wanted to make money the easy way, without working nine to five. And now he finds himself in this sticky predicament.

We met on the boardwalk of Rye Playland, a very quiet place during the off season. Phuc was a very slightly built man in his twenties. He was dressed in his chef garb and looked terrified.

"Hi Phuc, I'm Frankie Miranda. I understand you have some information for me."

It's important to achieve a rapport with any informant. Things will go a lot smoother if you build a sense of trust with the C.I. As we shook hands, I could feel him trembling. "Relax," I said, "this is gonna work out for the both of us."

"Phuc," I continued. "I'm on your side. If your guy proves to be what you say he is, then you'll stay out of jail. I promise."

Phuc appeared slightly relieved. "I've got a lot to offer you," he said.

"Who's the guy you're talking about?" I asked.

"He's an attorney. His name is Quan Ly. He helps lots of Vietnamese people who immigrate to the U.S. He has many connections in Ho Chi Minh City. He travels there several times a year. He can get you anything you want from the black market, drugs, guns, bombs and women. He has hundreds of people grateful to him for his assistance in relocating them to the U.S."

"How did you come to meet him?" I queried.

"During one of his trips to Saigon, he met my cousin Fabienne Do," he said. "She was only 18 and was Miss Saigon. Fabienne is so beautiful, he fell for her. So many men did. Quan Ly was just another in a long string of admirers." Phuc and I got a few more details of our story straight and were ready to rock and roll.

The meeting with Quan Ly was set for Tuesday at noon. We were to meet at Ly's Getty Square office in Yonkers. Ly has another office in Elmhurst Queens, New York, but I wanted the knucklehead on my turf. Phuc told

Quan that I was interested in sampling his coke. If the purity level was good, I'd buy an ounce to show good faith. I was instructed to bring $1,200 cash with me.

I was equipped with an audio / video transmitter. Angel was covertly recording it all from a nearby van. If the coke tested positive, I would give my usual buzz phrase "Break out the Champagne" cueing Angel to barge in and make the arrest.

Phuc and I entered Ly's office carrying a small black leather bag, containing chemical reagents and a few glass beakers. His secretary Jarrod, a thirty something guy, who reeked of cologne, gave us the go ahead to enter Quan Ly's inner office.

"Gentlemen, come in. You must be Frank. I see you came prepared," he quipped.

"You must be Mr. Ly," I replied.

"Frank, please call me Quan. Have a seat."

Ly was studying me from head to toe. Suspicious that I might not be who I say I am.

"So," Quan asked, "how do you and my little friend know each other?"

"We were in Sing-Sing State prison a few years ago," I said. "I went to Saigon Shack, in Nyack, last year to grab a bite and there he was, slaving away in the kitchen."

"What did you do time for Frank?" Quan asked.

"Armed robbery but I was only driving the get away car. I did five years for it. It was the biggest mistake of my life. From then on, I'm as careful as I can be."

"Yes Frank," he responded, "I am too. You can understand that, I'm sure."

Quan Ly went on, "The only reason I agreed to meet with you is because Phuc sang your praises. A man in my position can never be too careful. Phuc and I are like family."

"Understood," I replied.

Ly opened his desk drawer as Phuc and I looked on. He removed a small clear pouch of a white powdery substance and tossed it across his desk. "Let me know if you like it. There's a lot more where that came from."

I removed one of the beakers and the chemicals from my bag and placed them on the desk. I put some of the powder into the beaker. I poured a small amount of cobalt thiocyanate and an equal amount of hydrochloric into the beaker, waiting for a chemical reaction. All eyes were peeled on me. Bingo! The test proved positive for cocaine.

"Are you a chemist or something?" Quan asked.
I'm representing serious people," I scoffed. "I can't give them a product that's been cut five or six times." At this point I knew I had him in the bag. I handed him $1,200. He counted it and smiled.

"Nice doing business with you," Quan said. "Phuc said you're a multi- kilo guy."

I replied. "I'm also interested in buying sodium nitrate."

"Oh," Quan blurted out, "I guess my talkative little friend told you I dealt in sodium. I certainly don't keep it in the office."

Phuc sat there taking it all in. I noticed his knees were shaking. I hoped that Quan wouldn't pick up on it. "Quan," I said "we're gonna do a boatload of business together. Let's break out the champagne."

The charade was over. We laughed and made small talk for a few minutes. Suddenly, Jarrod yelled out, "You can't barge in there. Hey...."

Angel, gun drawn headed to Quan and shouted, "Police, you're under arrest!" Angel yanked him up from his chair and pulled Quan's arms back, cuffing him. Quan Ly looked to be in the state of shock. I handcuffed Phuc to make it look like he was innocent of the deception, but his role would be revealed to Quan's attorney at some point.

"Shit, wait minute guys," Quan Ly shouted, "can't we work out a deal? Just us, there's no need to take me in. My life is on the line here. Please!"

Quan Ly begged, "I can make you very rich men!"

"No dice," I huffed, "tell it to the judge."

Chapter Thirty-Seven

Quan Ly was in for the ride of his miserable life. He was anxiously waiting to be grilled in our interrogation room. It had been several hours since we first laid eyes on each other. I looked the same. He looked like a hit of cocaine could improve his mood.

"Listen," Ly cried out, "I'm having chest pains. Can't you see I'm in no condition to answer any questions? I need medical help."

All 200 pounds of Ly slumped back in his chair, his eyes rolled upwards and he was sweating profusely. Ly was in serious condition. Beau called 911 and Quan Ly was taken to White Plains Hospital. Our inquisition would have to wait.

The next morning Quan was subject to a hospital bed arraignment. He had suffered a drug withdrawal episode. He had been treated and was in stable condition, good enough to answer questions.

Beau decided to proceed with the questioning in the hospital. We took all the necessary paraphernalia to the hospital. Lights, camera, action! The camera was on and Ly was read his rights. The formalities were now out of the way. Quan anxiously said, "I don't want counsel. I'm a fucking lawyer. I know my rights. I'm gonna make the best deal for myself that I can. My life is ruined, my family destroyed." His eyes welled up, but no tears fell.

Beau began his spiel. "It's been established that you're a drug dealer. You are charged with felony sale of a controlled substance, namely cocaine. It's a charge that will end your law career if you are found guilty, you will be disbarred. However, if you cooperate and assist us in our endeavors to catch some bigger fish, things may improve for you. There are certain people who deal in illicit explosive materials. We have our sites set on them. Your cooperation will be vital in apprehending them or anyone like them. If the information is fruitful, we'll highly recommend clemency from the court at sentencing and request no jail time. This is not a promise, just a very strong possibility."

Quan was all ears. He answered, "What options do I have? None. These guys I deal with are dangerous and will seek revenge if they think I sang. They are Chinese racketeers. They show no mercy."

Beau replied abruptly, "We can offer you and your family the Witness Protection Program. We'll do everything in our power to protect your anonymity. That's all we can offer you Mr. Ly. Now tell us all about them."

Quan Ly thought for a moment and said, "It's the same guy who supplies me with drugs, Tommy Chen. He's all about the money. He deals in anything you can think of; ammonia nitrates, sodium nitrates, blasting agents, you name it. I've witnessed him sell two barrels of malathion to some Arabs."

"Malathion?" Beau questioned.

"It's an insecticide, you can cook it down to produce sarin gas," Quan Ly responded.

I interrupted and yelled, "Did it ever occur to you they might be terrorists? I guess it's all about the money, right!"

Beau continued, "Would you recognize these Arabs if I showed you a photo?"

"Maybe," Ly said.

I threw Hani's mug shot in front of Ly's fat bloated face. "It's hard to say,the two guys I saw both wore beards."

Now double teaming Ly, Beau hit him with another pertinent question. "Who is Chen's supplier? Where does he get the drugs and chemicals from?"

"Tommy Chen is a self made millionaire," Ly said. "Tommy owns a chain of elite restaurants, "House of Chen." He travels on his private jet between Hong Kong, New York, Vegas and California to manage them. He supplements his earnings by dealing drugs and arms. It's never enough for him. I don't know his sources."

"Okay, Quan," Beau said, "here's what we're gonna do. Frank is going to pose as an international arms dealer looking for explosives for his clients. You'll arrange an introduction to Chen."

"Do I have a choice?" murmured Ly.

"No! Now let's get down to business," replied Beau.

Chapter Thirty-Eight

I met with our tech guy, Detective Steve Skowronski, to discuss my best options for the buy of my lifetime. He suggested I wear a high tech HD3 Slyde wrist watch that records day or night, has tremendous resolution, coupled with his new favorite gadget, a cross pendant necklace body cam. I liked the idea of using both of them. The cross will only record for two hours and the watch will continue to pick up anything in excess of that. I was anxious to get this show on the road; the road to Fort Lee, New Jersey. Matthews reached out to his counterpart in Fort Lee. We had the probable cause to search Tommy Chen's house. Some of the detectives from the New Jersey State Prosecutor's Office will assist in the sting, buy/bust. I was scheduled to purchase 30 grand worth of drugs and bomb making components.

Quan Ly and I headed to Fort Lee, a bedroom community that has been called New York City's sixth borough. The large majority of its populous works in Manhattan. Tommy Chen had purchased himself a luxury home, perched on a hillside looking across the Hudson River to New York City.

Quan Ly and I arrived at Hawks Nest, Chen's aptly named house, about 7 p.m. Angel and the Jersey cops were safely in place nearby, waiting for my signal to execute the warrant. Quan rang the doorbell. Tommy Chen opened the door. Quan Ly made the introduction. "Tommy, this is Frankie Miranda, the guy I was telling you about. Frankie, meet Tommy Chen."

We sealed our introduction with a firm handshake. Chen was not what I expected. He was over 6-feet tall, mid thirties, slender and meticulously groomed. He wore white skinny jeans, an Hermes belt and a white cashmere V neck sweater and red velvet Gucci loafers.
"Welcome, gentlemen, come in," Tommy said. "How have you been Quan? It's been awhile."

"I'm good Tommy," Quan replied, "You?"

"Fine, as you can see." Tommy smirked and gestured to the grandeur of his surroundings.

Hawks Nest was a smaller version of Tony Stark's residence in the movie *Ironman*. Glass, glass and more glass. A stunning work of architecture. We entered Chen's sitting room, it was decorated in total modernist style with Asian accents. The focal point of the sitting room was a huge built-in fish tank.

"Ah, Frank," Tommy said, "I see you've noticed my treasured fish. My Chinese Red Dragonfish. Aren't they beautiful? I had to use my connections in the *Fish Mafia* to acquire them. Yes, there really is such a thing! They are the most desired salt water aquarium fish in the world. They bring me continued prosperity and luck."

"Very interesting," I remarked. "I could use a few myself," I chuckled.

"They're much more than a hobby to me," Chen explained. "You're looking at half a million dollars in luck. They come at a high price. We Chinese believe that a feng shui aquarium with 9 Red Dragonfish attracts wealth and abundance. I try to do most of my East Coast business in this room."

Chen poured each of us a scotch. "I was born in the Gansu Province, one of the poorest in China. Our region had little water and less work. As a little boy, I survived by eating bitter weeds for nourishment."

Quan interrupted and laughed as he spoke. "As they say, you've come a long way baby!"

"Yes," Tommy went on, "now my mother can live like a fine lady in retirement. She is the inspiration for everything I have ever done to get us out of Gansu." He gestured to a picture set on a pearly white Baby Grand of himself and his mother, Qui Chi.

"Well done my friend," said Quan Ly.

We all clicked glasses in agreement.

"Now let's get down to business," said Tommy.

"Quan, are you okay?" Chen asked. "You look a little pale."
"I'm just getting over the flu," Quan lied. Quan motioned for more scotch, Chen poured.

"My trusted friend Quan Ly vouches for your honor Frank," Chen remarked.

"Tommy, I need some sodium nitrate and some blasting caps. Can you accommodate me?" I asked.

Chen smiled and said, "Frank, of course I can accommodate you. It's $80 a kilo. I can get sodium nitrate by the ton from one of my Asian sources. The black powder based nitro-carbo blasting caps will cost you $50 per cap. These are very competitive prices. I understand you're interested in buying cocaine as well."

"Absolutely," I shot back. I chugged down my scotch. "The coke will depend on price and quality."

Tommy replied, "My product is top quality. No compromises there. It's worth 30k per kilo. As a courtesy to Quan Ly, I'll reduce the first purchase to 28k. Subsequent purchases will be negotiable."

"You understand I need to test it first," I said. "I gotta see what I'm buying."

"I gotta see the cash," laughed Chen.

Chen led us through an enclosed portico to his garage. There were two Chinese Shar-Pei dogs guarding the entrance to the garage. They growled fiercely as we approached. Tommy calmed them down and locked them in their cage. We entered the three car garage. Chen had a small room behind a false wall where he hid his wares. Tommy used his fingerprint to open the biometric lock on the safe. He removed two packages. One was coke, the other sodium nitrate. I spotted three barrels labeled malathion in the corner of the room. I pointed over and asked, "What's that?"

"Insecticide," Tommy replied. "Let's go back inside."

"Insecticide?" I questioned.

"Yes," Tommy responded. "When it's cooked down by 50%, it becomes sarin gas. Don't worry; in its present state it's harmless."

We resettled in the sitting room. Chen, pointed to the coke sitting on a marble coffee table and said, "The cocaine is 86% pure, taste it." "I prefer to test it," I said.

It tested positive for cocaine. "I'll take the coke, you take the cash. We've got a deal"

As I was about to give the pre-arranged arrest signal "Break out the champagne" a shot rang out, breaking through the glass window wall, shattering it. Startled, the three of us ducked for cover. There were glass shards everywhere. More gunshots torpedoed in from the yard. I tried to see where the gunfire was coming from but didn't raise my head for fear of being obliterated. Who was the target, me, Tommy Chen, Quan Ly? At the moment it didn't really matter. I just wanted to survive. I wanted to live through the night. Another quick succession of rounds from an automatic weapon eviscerated what remained of the glass walls. Tommy and Quan Ly took off running. That last burst of gunfire fractured the fish tank. The sound of breaking glass echoed everywhere. A 500 gallon waterfall cascaded onto the floor of the once tranquil sitting room. The nine chili reds, two-foot long Dragonfish were flopping all over the floor. They leaped through the air like daredevil Evil Knievel jumping 50 cars on his motorcycle. Within minutes, I heard a voice over a bullhorn, "Police, drop your weapons, hands up!" Cops had swarmed the scene entering through large jagged openings that were windows moments ago. A volley of shots continued. Then there was total silence. There was a momentary calm after the chaos. The detectives rushed in and secured the crime scene. "You alright Frankie?" Angel asked.

"Yeah, I'm soaking wet, but okay," I replied as I got up from behind the couch, brushing some of the fragments of glass from my clothes.

"You're better off than him," Angel replied.

The little boy from Gansu Province had run out of good fortune. In a frantic effort to flee, Tommy must have slipped on the wet Carrera marble on the sitting room floor. His jugular vein was severed by a sharp fragment of glass from the fish tank. He bled out in a few minutes. According to his culture, given the life he led, he will likely be a hungry ghost in the netherworld for all eternity. In the mêlée, the photograph of Tommy Chen and his beloved mother poetically landed on the floor next to him. His dead eyes were open, staring at the picture.

"What the hell happened, Angel? Who started shooting?" I barked.

"We heard shots fired," Angel replied. "One of the detectives spotted someone dressed in military style camouflage gear taking aim into the house. A firefight ensued, the rest is history. There he is out back, spread eagle on the grass. His 300 Winchester Magnum rifle lay next to his lifeless body. Frankie, there was a second shooter who escaped."

"Did you get Quan Ly?" I asked.

Angel shook his head. "No sign of him anywhere."

The dead man behind the house was identified as Teddy Urso. Teddy was an enforcer for the Lucheses and no stranger to working for Nick Galgano. Apparently, Urso's first shot took out Tommy Chen's bodyguard, who secretly waited on the patio by the rear door.

Did Nick have inside information that I'd be here tonight and commission Teddy to kill me? Sure looks that way. The Jersey detectives did a room by room search of Hawks Nest. The safe was peeled open by one of their safe cracking experts. We confiscated six more kilos of cocaine, the rest of the sodium nitrate and blasting caps, along with three barrels of malathion. Then we hit the mother-load, a ledger was found in the safe. It contained a treasure trove of information about purchases of illicit materials. One buyer's name stuck out like a sore thumb, Mustafa Salib. Mustafa had an asterisk next to his name. The itemized account showed that he bought cocaine and malathion from Tommy Chen. Either Mustafa wanted the malathion to make their lawn greener or he wanted to produce sarin gas. I'll go with the latter. We know that Salib is on Homeland Security's Terrorist Watch List. We now know where he was getting his bomb making materials. We just need to find him. The body cam footage was taken into evidence for future reference, but at a quick glance, it appeared to be of no benefit.

Chapter Thirty-Nine

DA John Xavier Hogan had been briefed and called a meeting for the next morning. The office was on fire with talk of the events of last night. Lingering questions needed to be answered. Hogan began the meeting, "Folks, your safety is my main concern. I'm relieved everyone on our side came out of this mess unscathed. Frank, you were in the line of fire. The good Lord was with you last night."

"Yes sir He was," I smiled gratefully.

This meeting was an opportunity for me to reveal that I had information that there was a mole in the office. One who likely tipped off Galgano to my meeting with Tommy Chen in New Jersey. I was bursting to shout it out but decided to control my impulse to spill the beans.

Hogan pressed on. "Does anyone here know why Teddy Urso, a known hit man for the mob, would be positioned outside Chen's house? We need to find out the motive behind the shootings and his intended target. Quan Ly is apparently on the lam and may hold the key to the attempted murder. I'm making this investigation a top priority. Work together on this and get results quickly. Now excuse me, I've got to deal with the press hounds clamoring for more information. Meeting adjourned."

As everyone started to file out of Hogan's office, I held back a bit. "Mr. Hogan," I said, "I need to have a meeting in private with you ASAP."

He didn't hesitate to say, "Back here in one hour."

Hogan and I reconvened at 11:15 a.m. "Sit down Frank. What did you want to see me about?"

"Mr. Hogan," I said, "I was privy to some information that I feel that I will only divulge to you. I have an irrefutable confidential source who told me that we have a mole in this office. It's someone that Nick Galgano has under his thumb. I suspect that this spy has been leaking information for some time. Galgano wants me dead, it's no secret. I believe I was the intended target in New Jersey and in the shooting of Joe Nulligan."

Hogan was riveted on my every word. "Who is your source? Are you 100% sure the allegation is correct?"

"Sir, I'm 100% sure," I said. "I'm not comfortable releasing the name of the informant. I took the information in confidence."

"Okay, Frankie," he replied. "Let's work together and uncover who's selling us out! God only knows what kind of critical information is being spilled. The office is under a dark cloud until we find the mole. Thank you for coming to me."

That afternoon, Joe was being released from the hospital. We cops stick together like white on rice. A brigade of cops dressed in their pressed blues were on hand in the hospital plaza as Joe left the hospital, cheering him on with applause. Teary eyed, he shook his head in thankfulness for the support.

I drove Joe and Jessica to their apartment on Garth Road in Scarsdale, New York. It was a long, quiet ride. Joe stared out the side window the entire thirty minutes. He rudely answered our questions with a grunt or two. He was in no mood to socialize. When we arrived, I asked Joe if he needed help getting up to his apartment. "No thanks," he replied in a stern voice. "I'll be fine," he growled.

The next day, Joe agreed to have lunch with me at his place. I showed up at noon, with some takeout from his favorite place, A Slice of Scarsdale Pizza.

Joe answered the door in his robe and slippers. He appeared to have started a liquid lunch, or maybe breakfast, prior to my arrival. He sat down in his recliner and positioned his shoulder so he was comfortable. He was clearly schnookered. "Grab yourself a drink, Frankie," he said twisting his words around his tongue.

"Okay, thanks," I replied. "Looks like you already grabbed a few."

"Yep, I'm an invalid," he said slurring his words, "I got nothing better to do."

"Joey, you gotta give it some time. Things are gonna improve," I said trying to reassure him. "We're all here for you."
"Don't give me that shit," he yelled, "I know better."

"Listen Joe, try to stay positive. You've been traumatized. You've got a lot going for you. Take it one day at a time."

"I know you're right Frankie. What if I can never work again? Huh? The doctors said mine was one of the most severe cases they had treated" he grunted.

"Like I said Joe, one day at a time." I bent down and gave him encouraging hug. "I'll try to stop by tomorrow, okay? Get some rest. More rest, less booze."

Joe forced a smile and said, "See ya tomorrow, Frankie boy."

Chapter Forty

Ace had obtained information from a C.I. that Ayman Hani hangs out at
a Middle Eastern grocery on West 38th Street in NYC. We decided to
try our luck and meet there. The Little Beirut Grocery was a run down
excuse for a store. A bevy of old men rustled around in the front entry.
We made our way past them into the store. The shelves had the usual
Middle Eastern foods stocked. Ayman Hani shoved his face through an
opening in a pair of curtains covering the backroom entrance. He spotted
me and took off. Guns drawn, we ran after him. He quickly zipped out
the back door and into an alley. A woman took off with him. Midway
in the alleyway she and Hani did an abrupt about face and began
pumping bullets at us! Ace and I dove for cover behind a garbage
dumpster. I don't know about Ace, but I've been shot at enough. My
quota is maxed out!

The perps ran out into the street and disappeared. Ace and I cautiously
pursued them but they were no where to be found. Rather than wait
around for NYPD to show up, we decided to get into our cars and leave
the area. There were too many questions we didn't want to answer right
now and we were both physically exhausted. We decided to regroup at
Emeril's new Italian Classic Restaurant on East 79th Street. Maybe
some of Chef Emeril's food could ease our nerves. The hostess greeted
us with a warm smile and a hello. Little did she know the harrowing
afternoon we just had. We took a small quiet back booth, away from the
crowd. Before we sat, we asked the hostess to send back two Glenlivets
on the rocks. We needed to calm ourselves down. Enough is enough.

Ace calmly said, "Cheech, you know we almost got killed back there."
"Tell me about it," I replied. "These motherfuckers mean business, but
what the degenerate bastards don't know is who the hell they're fucking
dealing with!"

I railed on and said, "You know the bitch who escaped with Ayman Hani looks like the one I saw outside White Plains Hospital the day Joey got shot."

"Two more Glenlivets neat," I yelled to the server.

We were too unnerved to order food yet. We simply sat making mad love to our scotches till we regained some normalcy. We sat, drank and finally ate. Three hours had passed. It was time to head out. Ace and I shook hands reconfirming our alliance against the pricks that are making this beautiful world an ugly and dangerous place.

On the ride home, I informed C.J. Matthews of our run in Hani and his female companion. "Captain, we spotted them but the suckers got away," I lamented.

"Let's meet first thing," C.J. replied.

I got home and Denise was in bed reading a murder mystery. She loves cops and robbers stuff. I can't go near those books, too fake. I crashed till the next morning.

Chapter Forty-One

I wasn't able to get a lot of sleep last night. Being shot at tends do that to you. This morning I'm determined to keep calm and carry on.

C.J. Matthews briefed us about a major theft that took place last night. A chemical manufacturing plant in upstate New York, near the Canadian border was broken into and robbed of six, fifty gallon drums of malathion. "Frankie, as you already know," C.J. said, "Malathion is a component in the manufacturing of sarin gas. The State Police theorize that the malathion is heading our way." Sometimes when you're so involved, you can't see the forest for the trees and maybe Little Beirut Grocery would yield more fruit. I decided to take a second look at the place.

Denise and I were now like two ships passing in the night. Usually when she was walking into the apartment, I was walking out. Today was no different. She wasn't feeling well and decided to stay home from work and nurse the flu. I gave her a peck on the cheek before leaving the apartment. As soon as I started the Vette, I turned on the portable police radio to the chatter of detectives in the field talking to one another about locations they were surveilling and when they'd be returning to the office.

In 30 minutes I arrived at the grocery store. I parked up the street and began to watch the foot traffic in and out of the store, hoping that Hani or the woman, who I believed was Zharkov, would walk in. I'd been sitting on the store for an hour and my eyes were getting tired. I saw someone that I recognized walk into the store. It was Arturo Colona, an old informant of mine. The little doper fought like a junk yard dog when I locked him up several years ago for possession of coke. After some forceful persuasion, Arturo decided to cooperate with my office to save his ass from going to jail. Short and wiry, weighing less than 150 pounds, with jet black hair, this native Columbian, gave me what was proven to be the biggest cocaine bust in Westchester County history. He set up a couple of New Jersey drug dealers, Gilberto and Julia Gomez, Columbian Nationals who thought that they were selling 15 pounds or seven kilos of pure blow to a wise guy, Frank Miranda, who turned out to be me. At the time, the drugs had a street value of three million dollars.

The Gomez's arranged for two Columbian mules to deliver the cocaine from their home in Union City to a low rent apartment in Yonkers. The Gomez's plan was to drive to a New Main Street apartment in Yonkers, wait in the apartment for the sale to go down and then collect their money. At the time of the transaction, Arturo and I had no idea that the Gomez's brought most of the cocaine in the Yonkers apartment.

The mules arranged to meet us at the Dew Drop Inn, in Elmsford, NY to sell one kilo of the coke and then bring the money back to the Yonkers apartment. Once the Gomez's felt secure with the first sale, they would have the mules sell the rest of the drugs. What the mules didn't expect was to be arrested after the first sale went down. When confronted with the proposition of spending the rest of their lives in prison, they agreed to cooperate with my office. They said that Gilberto and Julia were waiting for them to return with the money in their nephew's apartment.

My command was notified of the arrests and that we were proceeding back to Yonkers. I had one of the mules call Gilberto from his cell phone and persuade him to come down to the parking lot to pick up the money. The bastard wouldn't budge from the apartment. The enforcement team, dressed in black jump suits, armed with shot guns and automatic rifles, wasted no time in knocking down the door with a steel battering ram. The door flew off its hinges into the nephew's living room. Gilberto's nephew was immediately knocked to the ground and handcuffed. Julia and Gilberto were in the kitchen trying to dump the rest of the cocaine out the window. After a brief struggle they were taken into custody and six kilos of cocaine were recovered. The two mules were held as material witnesses and testified against Julia and her husband at trial.

The outcome of their trial wasn't pretty but it was just. They were both convicted. Julia received 15 years to life and Gilberto got 18 years to life in State Prison. In exchange for their testimony, the mules lucked out and were deported back to their country. Arturo and I lost touch when I started to work with Mike Baraka. Now it seems that he's back in the picture again and is on the other side of the law.

My eyes were glued on the front door, waiting for Arturo to leave. He didn't leave for thirty minutes and walked out carrying a brown leather briefcase. I eyed him with binoculars, up the street to a Ford Mustang. I pulled away from the curb and accelerated to stay three cars behind him. He didn't seem to be looking for a tail. I followed him for fifteen minutes to Riverside Drive where he turned, made a sharp right turn and parked in front of 1172 East 181st Street in Washington Heights, a four story apartment building. He got out of the car carrying the briefcase and entered. After sitting on the building for a few minutes, a sliding glass door on the fourth floor balcony opened. Arturo and another male walked out onto the balcony. They were animated as they spoke and were in a heated discussion. Ace called. I must have sounded excited as I answered. I told him that I followed an old informant and what I had just observed. My next question to him was obvious. "Ace, does your department have any intelligence on the building?"

"Cheech," he said, "you must be psychic or something. It just landed on my desk. Look, our Bronx Organized Crime Control Bureau and the Vice Enforcement Division are planning to execute a search warrant on the fourth floor of that building tomorrow. I'll bet it's the same apartment that your guy is in. They're investigation; *Operation Jinn* has been going on for over a year now. It's a safe house where heroin is being cut, packed and distributed. They think the heroin is coming in from the Middle East. The judge wants the investigation ended and won't renew the eavesdropping orders."

I yelled into the phone, "No fucking shit! Ace, any idea whose operation it is?"

Ace replied, "Inspector Sean Rowland of Vice Enforcement thinks you have stumbled onto a hornet's nest. Mustafa Salib is the target of the investigation and it's believed that the heroin operation is his."

Damn, Arturo's in bed with these scumbags and he doesn't know it yet, but he's gonna take me right to them and bust my case wide open. I was emphatic when I told Ace that I want to be there when they raid the apartment. Before he clicked off the call, he cautioned me, "I gotta tell you that this information is confidential. Bronx Vice Enforcement has wire taps up all over the city and lower Westchester."

My mind was running like a run-away freight train. I wondered if Ayman Hani and Anna Zharkov were involved with Salib. Moments later, Colona hurried out of the building and was no longer carrying the briefcase. Before he got into his car, he eyed the street suspiciously. Like the old saying goes, "A leopard doesn't change his spots." So, this misfit was back in the drug business. I'll bet ya dollars to donuts that there was drug money in the briefcase he carried in. What Arturo doesn't know is that I am back in his life. I followed him to Parkhill Avenue, Yonkers, New York. I found out that his car was registered there. I'd soon be paying the dirt bag a visit.

Chapter Forty-Two

It looked like the Army's third infantry division was ready to invade Washington Heights. I was sitting with Ace in his Ford Taurus waiting for the games to begin. The raiding party was a few blocks away gearing up. They were putting on bulletproof vests, raid jackets and readying their firearms. There were three armored vehicles, staffed by NYPD's Emergency Service, members from NYPD's Organized Crime Control Bureau (OCCB), Bronx Vice Enforcement and a number of agents from the FBI and Homeland Security. They were assigned in groups of two. Some were assigned to the rear of the building to prevent an escape and others were positioned in the alley separating the target location from the adjacent building. The entry team would gain access to the building through the front entrance, make their way to the fourth floor and knock apartment 4J's door down with a battering ram. This was war!

The armored vehicles started toward the building. They drove down the street, with the other teams following. Their main objective was to apprehend and arrest Mustafa Salib and at the very least, apprehend the people bagging heroin in the apartment.

In a matter of minutes all the units were in position to execute the no-knock warrant. Eyes have been on the building since 6:00 a.m. We were watching the comings and goings of people in an out looking for Salib. So far today, Mustafa Salib has not been seen. The powers that be hoped that Salib was in the apartment. No matter what, the plan was to execute the warrant at 3:30 p.m.

I commented, "Maybe Hani and Anna Zharkov are in the apartment?"
Ace shrugged and said, "Cheech, we'll know soon enough."
At exactly 3:30 p.m., the command to execute the warrant blared over the police radio. All the units rolled toward the building and positioned themselves to carry out the operation. Emergency Service cops dressed in

black assault fatigues piled out of the armored personnel carriers rushed into the building. The rest of the teams took up their assigned locations. You could hear the racket from the street as the cops made their way to the fourth floor. In a matter of seconds, three or four loud thuds were heard from the battering ram slamming into the door. A cluster of cops were heard screaming, "Hands up, get the fuck down on the floor!"

There was the sound of gun fire from automatic weapons ta-ta-ta-ta. The shooting lasted for about a minute.

Ace and I, our hearts raced like had damn epinephrine injections, rushed up the front stairs, into the building, up the four flights of stairs. The door to apartment 4J hung to one side. We bent over to suck in some air before scrambling into the apartment with our pistols drawn, and pointing down to the floor. We stepped over the body of a Middle Eastern male, dressed in an Arab tunic, who'd been shot in the face; half of his head was gone. Another dead body was in the corner of the living room. He had five bullet holes in his torso and his mouth hung open like he was trying to say something before he died. An automatic pistol lay beside him. They were armed, and shot by the Emergency Service cops as they entered the apartment. Another Middle Eastern guy in his early twenties was on the floor handcuffed to a radiator, he was later identified as Ezra Awad. We later found out that Awad had entered the country illegally, by way of Canada. Most likely he is one of Salib's underlings.

The apartment was sparsely furnished. A ten foot metal table sat in the middle of the living room. On top of the table was uncut heroin, cutting agents, scales and zip lock glassine bags for packaging with *Habibi* embossed on the bag. *Habibi* translated means beloved. I looked around the room for Hani and Anna Zharkov. I thought that the guy with no face might be Hani, but no such luck. The dead guy was later identified as Kareem Nabu, age 33, an illegal from Egypt. To everyone's disappointment Mustafa Salib wasn't in the apartment.

NYPD Captain Dennis McCleary, aka "The Silver Fox", a distinguished looking cop in his early sixties with silver gray hair, supervised the search of the apartment. Two officers were assigned to search each room, with one cop conducting the search and the other noting where evidence of a crime was found.

We were in the living room when one of the cops yelled out that there was a large amount of cash in the fridge's freezer. Over one million dollars was stashed there, no doubt the money was from the heroin sales that funded Salib's terrorist actions. Thousands of glassine bags, containing a gram of heroin, found hidden under a false floor under the kitchen sink were confiscated. *Habibi*, in bright blue letters was stamped on each bag. We believe that's Salib's brand name for the heroin he sells on the street. The drug is most likely smuggled into the country from Salib's connections in the Middle East. I'm sure that's why Salib chose it as his symbol on the package.

I stuck my head into one of the back bedrooms where detectives were boxing up a computer and its hard drive. The forensic imaging will hopefully yield a boondoggle of intelligence and hopefully stop any lethal attacks. Ezra Awad was brought out of the apartment in handcuffs by two EMS cops. He'll be interrogated but knowing these guys it's highly unlikely he will cooperate. It was just another day in paradise for Ace and me.

Chapter Forty-Three

Chief Larry Christopher called me into his office to discuss the raid in Washington Heights.

"Fill me in Frankie, you've had a busy week," Larry said.

"Yes I have Chief," I replied. "It's been one surprise after another. By the way, are you feeling okay? You look like you may be coming down with something. Ya know that wicked flu strain is going around."

"No, I feel fine," Larry huffed, "I still have some back pain from my ski injury."

No matter what he said, he looked like crap. Bloodshot eyes, droopy lids and weight loss, I've worked narcotics long enough to know that the dude was on something. I sat there filling him in on the week's events.

I decided that this was a good time to confront him about his daughter Liz. "Chief," I said, "I'm in an awkward spot here."

"Awkward spot?" he shot back, "what do ya mean?"

"You remember the Carroll Street investigation. I saw someone I recognized there. The surveillance photos confirmed my suspicions. It was Liz, your daughter, Chief. She entered the building and soon after staggered out. I kept the information to myself, but now I feel I need to share it with you."

Larry's eyes widened. Indignantly, he replied, "Yes, keep it to yourself. She's got a problem that we're trying to deal with. Like I said, stay the hell out of this. I don't need any damn help from you. Got it?"

I thought to myself. *Really chief! You behave like a delinquent child and look like shit. You've missed three important meetings this month alone and Hogan isn't pleased. Your wife drinks too much, your daughter is a drug addict and you say that you don't need help. Something is wrong with this picture.*

"Yes, sir," I replied. "I guess we're done here." I abruptly left him sitting there.

Later that afternoon, Joe Nulligan reluctantly agreed to meet with me and Tyra. We stopped by Garth Road for a quick social call. Jessica was at work. We knocked on his door several times.

"Come on in, it's open," he yelled.

"Hey buddy, since when do you leave your door unlocked?" I questioned.

"Since I'm too drunk to get up and fucking answer it," he laughed. "Get yourselves a drink," he slurred.

Tyra and I exchanged concerned glances.

"No thanks Joe," Tyra said. "I can't speak for Frank, but I'll pass."

"Me too," I said. "Just stopped by to see how you're doing."

We were just about to give Joe "the talk" when he passed out in the chair, snoring like a hibernating grizzly bear. Joe was losing hope of ever regaining a normal life. We quietly let ourselves out. I planned to discuss the situation at length with Jessica. As we drove away from Joe's apartment, Ace called. All he would say was that he had a situation in Tompkins Square Park in Manhattan.

Tyra and I arrived in Alphabet City, as it's sometimes referred to, in the East Village in NYC. We parked between Avenue A and B. Tompkins Square Park is a 10 acre parcel that has a rich history in Manhattan's development. In the 1600s, Peter Stuyvesant, a Dutch colonial governor, gifted the land to NYC for use as a public space. By the 1960s, it had become synonymous with increased social problems like protests and drug abuse. By the 1980s, encampments of homeless prevailed.

We spotted Ace and what looked to be crime scene near some benches. An ambulance and several patrol cars were parked nearby.

"What the hell happened here Ace?" I asked.

"We have another casualty of the drug war. We lost this battle," Ace said sullenly. "This one is way too close to home."

EMS specialists were just about to carry away a body bag. Ace said, "Her driver's license identifies her as Elizabeth Christopher. There was a note in her wallet that said, "In case of emergency contact Chief Lawrence Christopher." Ace hesitated a moment and said, "It's his daughter. I've been trying to reach him."

Tyra looked down at the body bag and said, "Holy shit."

"Can I take a look at her?" I asked.

Ace unzipped the bag to expose her abscessed face. "That's Liz," I said. I took a deep breath and exhaled slowly. She had a bluish hue.

"Needle Park" as Tompkins Square Park is referred to, is no stranger to homeless junkie *crusties*. They shoot up right in front of you. There's a colony of squatters that take up residence on benches and snooze in sleeping bags or on cardboard boxes. All sizes, ages and ethnicities, drug addiction crosses all social boundaries, mostly city dwellers here but the occasional rich kids from New Canaan and Westport, Ct. railroad in to see the sights and indulge in their favorite narcotic cocktail. Now Larry and Alice Christopher would suffer the staggering loss of Liz in Tompkins Square Park. Peter Stuyvesant would turn over in his grave twice!

As Liz's body was placed into the ambulance, I called Captain Matthews and gave him the grim news. He had to hunt down Larry.

She said, "Larry is coming apart at the seams as it is, after this tragedy, who knows how he'll fare."

"You're right Tyra," I replied. "I recently found him on the floor of the men's bathroom practically unconscious."

"Wow," she responded, "was he drunk?" "I couldn't tell," I said, "but he was clearly impaired."

We were knocked out from the days events and we were not looking forward to the next few days.

Chapter Forty-Four

Liz Christopher's wake was held at the Howard E .Campbell Funeral Home
on New York City's Upper East Side. An entourage from the DA's office
attended the evening viewing. The family decided on a one day wake
followed the next day by a funeral mass at the majestic neo-gothic St.
Patrick's Cathedral on Fifth Avenue.

The wake was as expected solemn and sad. Larry and Alice greeted visitors
near the coffin with tears and hugs. The Christopher's mettle will be tested
to the fullest in the aftermath of this dreadful tragedy.

Denise and I approached the grieving couple and offered them our
condolences. Larry pulled me close and whispered, "This is my fault
Frankie." He collapsed in my arms. I steered him to a front row seat and
tried to comfort him. "This is no one's fault Chief. No ones."

It was less than two days ago that I confronted Larry about Lizzie. Now,
here he is brokenhearted over his loss. My heart went out to him and Alice.
Short of wrangling Lizzie into rehab, there was little more a parent could do
to help the poor souls lost to drug addiction.

The next morning the procession continued from the funeral home to St.
Patrick's Cathedral, "America's Parish Church." The Christopher's were
devout Catholics and planned the mass and burial in traditional Catholic
fashion. Cardinal Malachi Xavier Hogan, DA John Xavier Hogan's older
brother celebrated the mass. Cardinal Hogan was an imposing figure with a
powerful presence, not unlike his little brother Johnny. Clearly the Hogan's
were a gifted family. Good looks and magnetism abounded. It was
rumored that Malachi will be the next Archbishop of New York. After
delivering an eloquent eulogy, Cardinal Hogan led the convoy up to
Calvary Cemetery in Westchester. After a brief graveside prayer, mourners
were lulled by the dulcet tones of Amazing Grace, performed by the Police

Emerald Society Bagpipers. We then bid our farewells to little Elizabeth Christopher. Go into peace with God, Liz.

Denise, Tyra, Joe, Jessica, Angel and a few others congregated at Jake's after the burial. We shot the usual shit, but with a somber overtone, a typical Irish wake. Eventually, we laughed and cajoled one another till it was closing time. Each of us wondering, who would be the next to go.

Chapter Forty-Five

Identity theft and credit card fraud impact millions of Americans each year. The thieves use this personal information to open bank and credit card accounts, file tax returns and get loans, wreaking havoc on the victim's lives. One of Richie's informants told him of a group of Arabs that are involved in such a scam. Their illegitimate earnings were suspected to be used for jihad operations in the United States.

Richie said that it might be a long shot, but this group of Arabs might be connected to the terror cell I was investigating. We also had an in-depth conversation about the raid on East 181st Street in Washington Heights. We both hoped that with some friendly persuasion, Ezra Awad would flip and put us in position to stop another major terrorist attack. I advised Richie that the hard drive seized might provide intelligence as to where Salib is shacked up. As an added bonus, I told my brother about my chance observation of my old informant Arturo Colona. Colona had no idea that I knew he was selling heroin for Salib. Richie said curiously, "I know you Frankie, when are you planning to sink your teeth into Colona?"

"Soon brother, soon," I said with a mountain of determination in my voice.

I thought about stopping by Jake's but I decided to put my time to better use and swing by Arturo's apartment to see if the son of a bitch was home. If he was, I just might pay him a visit.

I drove past the multi family house on Parkhill Avenue and sure enough, his red Mustang was parked out front. It was dusk and all three floors were lit up in the wood framed structure. The Parkhill Avenue is a quiet residential neighborhood in South Yonkers. The street is peaceful at the moment but that can all change in an instant.

I sat in the car for a minute and decided, what the hell, I'm gonna knock on the motherfuckers' door. I'd slipped the gun that I kept under the front seat into my waist. I gave my 9mm a friendly pat as I walked a few feet and climbed three sets of cement steps to the front door. I stepped into the foyer that leads into the dwelling. In the foyer were tarnished brass mail boxes with the tenants name and their apartment numbers inserted at the bottom. Arturo lived in apartment D, on the first floor. Each apartment had an intercom system requiring that the tenant buzz you in. Fortunately, someone was leaving the building and opened the door. I slipped in.

Arturo and I were going to get reacquainted and have a serious talk about life, especially his. I pulled out my gun and banged on the door with the butt of the gun. Arturo shouted, "Who is it?" I banged again. He slowly cracked the door open and saw that it was me. He tried to slam the door shut, but I hit the door with my shoulder, breaking the chain lock and forcing the door open. I didn't give the weasel a chance to run. I was all over him like a fox on a rabbit. I grabbed him by the nape of the neck and shoved him against the wall, shouting, "Surprise, surprise, motherfucker!" Slowly, I pulled him off the wall and forced him down on a moth-eaten sofa. He must have cut the back of his head when he hit the wall. Blood drizzled onto his neck, staining his tee-shirt. He ranted, holding his neck, putting pressure on it to stop the bleeding. "Frank what? What's this all about?"

I stood over him, the business end of the gun pointing down toward his head. "It's about you dealing heroin, you piece of shit! It's about all the people who die because of the poison you sell. It's about 181st Street! It's about Mustafa Salib! It's about Anna Zharkov and about fucking Ayman Hani! That's what this is about!"

He was literally collapsed leaning over, his shoulders hunched, his head dropped to his mid-section and he began shaking. He gasped and said, "Frank! What do you want from me? I....I..."

I didn't give him a chance to speak, talking over him. "I want Hani! I want the whole fucking bunch of them! I don't give a rat's ass about your heroin dealing! You're fucking working for me again. Ya understand?"

He looked up at me, fear imprinted on his face as he continued wiping blood from his neck as it seeped down his back. "Frank, they're dangerous people. I don't want to get myself killed."

The adrenaline pumped through me like water through a hose. I exploded. "You gotta worry about me, you fucking fuck! You gotta worry about spending the rest of your life in the can! That's what the fuck you gotta worry about!"

On top of a folding table were a number of small plastic bags stamped Habibi that contained a white powdery substance. Betcha the bags were filled with heroin that this son of a bitch was peddling. He got the shit from Salib.

I grabbed his wrist and twisted it back. He let out a muffled yell, "Ouch!" I motioned with my head toward the table, "What the fuck is that?" That could put you in the joint for a long, long, time. It's in plain view and you invited me in. Capisci?"

He tried to get up, but I shoved him back down. I shouted, "I didn't tell you that you could get up!" He was panting for air and stared down at the floor. He was afraid to look at me. "Look at me when I talk to you!" I said. "Look at me!" His eyes transfixed on mine. "That's better," I yelled. "Just so we have an understanding. You go about your business of peddling junk, but I want you to tell me everything that you know about Mustafa Salib. Ya know, my partner Joe was shot and someone tried to blow me up. Just so you get my drift."

The son-of a bitch sat silent for a moment. "Okay, okay," he cried. "I'll tell ya what I know, but ya gotta keep me out of it. They'll kill me if they find out I'm talking to you."

"Yeah, yeah," I said. I knew he didn't have a choice. He had to talk to me. "C'mon Arturo, start unloading."

"I've met this Hani at Little Beirut Grocery. He's been keeping a low profile. He knows that you and the FBI are looking for him. The guy's fucking evil. Hani's an important part of Mustafa's cell. Mustafa loves him. Hani believes in Jihad. I think he's blinded by the extremist ideology of Sharia Law. He's intent to destroy everything non-Muslim. Mustafa is grooming him for a higher position in his cell of fanatics."

Arturo looked like he was having second thoughts about talking. I poked him the chest and said, "Look, I said you gotta give me everything. Where's he crashing? I gotta find him and Hani. They're planning to gas a lot of innocent people."

His hands shook, his face ashen grey, as he nervously twitched and said, "Yeah, yeah, okay, but I can't do jail time. Ya gotta promise me."

"You give me Hani and Mustafa. I can promise you'll never see the inside of prison," I said sternly.

Arturo thought about it for a while and lamented, "Ya know, I've been peddling a lot of dope for Mustafa. He trusts me. He told me that he inherited a lot of money from his grandfather Usman who was a notorious bomb maker in Syria. Usman was the greatest single influence on him. Usman insisted that Salib live his life as a jihadist and carry on the family struggle. Mustafa's grandfather, Usman, had only 2 fingers remaining on his right hand at the time of his sudden death. Ezra Awad once mentioned to another jihadist that Mustafa killed his own grandfather, Usman."

162

I took note of what he just said. Killed his grandfather, huh.

"Remember Arturo, you can run, but you can't hide from me," I said in a threatening tone. "I want to know where he and the rest of the vermin are hanging their turbans and details on his next attack."

Arturo was worn out. I gave the prick a pass to deal heroin, as they say, sometimes you have to make a deal with the devil to get what you want.

Chapter Forty-Six

Tyra and I were assigned to a double homicide case. We were scheduled to meet with Angel's cousin, Detective Jorge Feliciano of the Harrison, NY, PD at the Westchester County Medical Examiners Office. Jorge was a handsome, young cop, raising two small daughters alone. "Jorge, what happened here?" Tyra asked as she motioned to two corpses lying on autopsy tables.

Jorge replied, "Two teenaged Hispanic girls were brutally beaten and murdered by some fiend. We are here to witness their autopsies. Hopefully their autopsies will shed some light on who killed them and why."

Jorge continued, "The bodies were tossed away like trash on the side of the road in Harrison. Department of Highway workers discovered two heavy duty garbage bags containing the victims, yesterday while cleaning a storm drain."

"How old do you think they were?" Tyra asked.

"Maybe seventeen or eighteen," Jorge replied. "It's hard to say."

Dr. Elizabeth Mungo, a middle aged Haitian, was to perform the autopsies. As Dr. Mungo began to snip open the ribcage on one of the girls, Tyra felt faint and began to sway. She fainted into Jorge's arms. He carried her outside to a quiet area and rested her on a gurney. She came to quickly but was embarrassed that she passed out. Tyra said, "This is not my first rodeo, but the sight and smells in there overwhelmed me."

"I'll let you in on a little secret Tyra," Jorge said, "I collapsed and fell to the ground at my first autopsy. Nobody caught me. No wonder, I'm 6 feet 2 inches and 220 lbs. You on the other hand felt like a feather. " They both chuckled.

Tyra remained outside while Jorge and I witnessed the rest of the Jane Doe's autopsies. A gruesome scene compounded by the rancid odors. It could test anyone's fortitude.

"Once we have an I.D. on these girls," Jorge remarked, "we'll start canvassing neighborhoods. Right now there's no missing persons report fitting their description. Their fingerprints came up negative."

The autopsies revealed that the girls were sexually assaulted, beaten, incurred severe head trauma. One was strangled with some kind of ligature; she was three months pregnant, with a boy. Forensics will run any available DNA in an attempt to find the demonic coward or cowards responsible for this horrific act.

Chapter Forty-Seven

Tyra and Jorge took the lead on solving the "West Street Murders." Their team was circulating photos of the victims everywhere and anywhere they could. They searched Manhattan, the Bronx, and up through Connecticut. Tyra said that she and Jorge handed out fliers with the girls photos in every bodega in the South Bronx. They showed the photos to a cashier in a bodega on East 149th Street and St. Ann's Avenue. The cashier not only recognized the missing girls, but knew them from the neighborhood. Norberto Barnes, the cashier, said that the girls were Daisy Soto and Felicity Dominquez, 15 and 16-years old respectively. The two were cousins who were closer than most sisters. Daisy and Felicity were truants from Mott Haven High School. They lived with Daisy's mother, Hilda Soto. Later that day, Jorge and Tyra were saddled with the grim task of notifying Hilda of the murders. Since Jorge was bilingual, he took the bull by the horns. Tyra said he spoke calmly in Spanish and with great compassion delivering the devastating news. Mrs. Soto stood frozen and then her knees gave way. Tyra said they tried their best to comfort her, but to no avail. Several neighbors ran into the apartment when Hilda began to wail. Tyra and Jorge decided to let her regain her composure before bombarding her with questions that needed answers.

"Mrs. Soto," Tyra said, "we'll be back later. Is there anything we can get you?" Hilda shook her head no.

Tyra and Jorge found a small luncheonette nearby. I met them for lunch. "All in a days work, right?" Jorge said dourly.

"It's part of what we do," Tyra said. "Sometimes the work really gets to you. This is one of those cases."

"I hear ya," I said shaking my head in agreement.

We were very hungry and devoured our arroz con pollo. We sat there and tried to socialize for a few minutes.

"Tell me a little about yourself, Jorge," Tyra asked.

"Long or short version?" Jorge chuckled.

"Somewhere in the middle," Tyra laughed.

"Okay. I'm Puerto Rico born. Wanted to be a cop as long as I can remember, graduated Pace University in New York. Joined the force. Married the love of my life, Dee Dee. Two kids."

"Sounds very fulfilling," Tyra replied, as she looked at me.

"It was more than perfect," Jorge said, "Until Dee Dee passed away giving birth to my youngest one, 4-year old Ava."

Tyra and I were taken aback hearing about his loss. "I'm so sorry Jorge," I said.

Frowning, Jorge continued, "They overdosed her with Pitocin. A drug used to escalate contractions during labor."

"How have you ever managed to juggle the children and your work?" Tyra asked.

"My mother and my mother-in-law saved the day," Jorge responded. "They have been nothing short of spectacular with Ava and 6-year old Tippy."

We finished eating and went back to Hilda's apartment. Hilda Soto lived on the 5th floor walkup of a rundown tenement building in the South Bronx. The elevated train ran 1000 feet parallel to her building. The noise was staggering when a train whizzed by. The building actually shook. The fire escapes were rusty and garbage was strewn all over the hall and stairs. Rats and roaches to follow.

We knocked on the apartment door. An older man answered the door. He led us through the dark hall to the living room where Hilda Soto awaited. "Mrs. Soto," I said, "I'm Detective Frank Santorsola from the Westchester County DA's Office. I'm very sorry for your loss."

Hilda didn't respond. She poured herself a glass of Don Q Rum, chug-a-lugged it and continued her catatonic stare. The old man said, "I'm Hilda's father, Esteban Camacho. I'm the girls' grandpapa."

"Mr. Camacho, I'm terribly sorry about the girls," Tyra said, "we all are."

"My daughter, Hilda, tried her best to raise Daisy on her own. Hilda's late husband, Umberto, was a mean SOB. He whipped Hilda and Daisy, especially when he was high on meth. A year ago, Hilda shot and killed Umberto in self defense. No charges were brought against her, except for the illegal gun. It has been more downhill since then. Daisy and Felicity started to run the streets. As you can see, Hilda's best friend, these days is Don Q. She didn't even know the girls were missing. I live in Mayaguez, Puerto Rico, most of the time. I'm too far away to be of any use. I have eleven kids. Seven are in Puerto Rico. Maybe Hilda will return with me."

Esteban continued to vent. "Look at how beautiful the girls were," pointing to a picture on the end table. "I took the photo at my house last summer. Two beautiful kids, full of life and promise. That devil not only killed my precious granddaughters, but my first great grandson as well. They told us Daisy was pregnant. He ended the baby's life too."

"It's so heartbreaking," Jorge remarked.

"Yes," Esteban said. "After Daisy's father died, the girls fell in with a wild crowd. You know, Daisy wanted to be another Jennifer Lopez. She never stopped dancing and singing. Felicity liked cosmetics and hairdressing. Any aspirations they had were devoured by their new found association with drugs."

Hilda, a bit lucid, said, "My beautiful girl. He did this to her. He did this. I warned her."

"Who did this, Mrs. Soto?" Jorge asked. "Please help us find the man who killed them."

"I don't remember who he is," Hilda wailed. "Daisy said she loved him. Love, what does a 15-year old know about love? She became a sex slave to him and his drugs. One night Daisy came home, she had two black eyes and her lip was cut. She told me that in a jealous rage, her boyfriend beat her. Felicity rescued her and got her home to safety."

"Please Mrs. Soto, you must know more about this guy!" Tyra pleaded.

"No I don't know nothing except he was a good looking man who cast a spell over my baby," Hilda cried. "Daisy told me she cast a Santeria spell over him to make him fall in love with her."

I asked, "Hilda, how would she do that? Who cast the spell? Who would know how to cast such a spell?"

Hilda replied. "The landlady. Jean Baptiste, for one, but there are many here in the South Bronx who dabble in Santeria."

"Okay," I said, "we're gonna let you good people rest for now. Take our business cards. If you think of anything that can help us, please call right away."

Jorge said his good byes in Spanish and we left.

"Where to now?" Tyra asked.

"The landlady," I replied.

We walked down five flights of stairs through the garbage to the superintendent's apartment. It was dark, dank and musty. We tried not to inhale too deeply. We rang the bell to the basement apartment door. The bell was broken, so we banged on the door several times. Finally a dark skinned petite woman in her eighties answered, she had a fat cigar hanging out of the side of her mouth.

"Police, ma'am, we have a few questions for you about the murders of Daisy Soto and Felicity Dominquez," Tyra said.

"An old lady like me got nothing to hide. Come in," she said in a thick Spanish accent.

"Are you Jean Baptiste?" Tyra asked.

"Yes, that's me," she replied. "Jean Baptiste de la Concepcion, first born child of Simon Derrick de la Concepcion."

Jean Baptiste is a Santeria Priestess. She wore a flowered tiara. Artificial red and yellow roses framed her weathered caramel colored face. Granny glasses and a long flowing flowered skirt completed the look.

"It's a shame about those two girls. I've known them since they were babies," Ms. de la Concepcion said with a scowl. "When you get to my age, you think you've heard it all. Then, whammy, this happened. I loved those two kids."

"Can you shed any light on the girl's murders?" Jorge asked.

"I can tell you that Daisy was madly in love with an older man. She said he only used her for sex, but she wanted him to love her back. She asked me to cast a Santeria love spell on him."

"She did!" Tyra blurted. "Exactly what does that entail?"

"Follow me," Jean Baptiste said. "I'll show you."

We followed her out to a dimly lit storage area adjacent her apartment. A few bicycles and shovels hid a secret door to a back room. Our mouths hung open as we gained entry to this Santeria prayer room! "Never saw anything like this," Tyra marveled.

There were several altars scattered around the room. "Oh here is Daisy's altar." Jean Baptiste pointed to it and said with pride, "Daisy's love altar was designed to bring her and her lover together."

On the altar was a red candle in the shape of a naked male. Next to it was the female counterpart. They were about a foot tall and had a wide base, the size of my hand. The candles were placed face to face. Pieces of apples, mushrooms, white bird feathers, religious candles and rose petals were arranged on a large tray. A tiny red felt bag with three stones was resting in the center of the altar.

Without interruption, Jean Baptiste said, "I placed two red candles together on the love altar, one in the image of a man, one in the image of a woman. I etched the names of the couple in the bottom of each. "See here," she pointed and lifted up the female candle. Daisy Soto's name was etched on the bottom. This was fascinating. This was the first time I encountered Santeria in the flesh.

"Ms. de la Concepcion," I interrupted, "who was the man she loved?"
She slowly flipped over the male candle. There it was in red and white,
much to our astonishment, it read Ayman Hani.

"Whoa," I shouted. "Are you fucking kidding me?"

We were dumbstruck. You could have blown us over with one of the
feathers. Our eyes never left Hani's name etched on the base of the candle.

"We need to take these candles. They're circumstantial evidence."

"Yes, I understand," she replied. "They are useless now and too sad to keep
around. I need room for the next hopefuls."

"Is there anything more you can assist us with?" I asked Jean Baptiste.
Shit, I thought the candles didn't do Daisy much good. "Thank you so
much," I continued, "you don't know how grateful we are to have this
information."

"You are very welcome," Jean Baptiste replied. "Don't forget my address if
you need a Santeria altar. The cost is $100 and they usually have very
satisfying results."

"We won't forget. Thank you," Tyra winked.

We started to walk back through the storage room, when we heard a loud
voice shriek out from the altar room. "Hey, hey, come back." Jean Baptiste
had one more card up her sleeve. "I almost forgot," she said, "I have one
more thing to show you."

We scurried back into the altar room. In the corner was a metal safety box.
It was surrounded by black candles burning in the dark room. A bit excited,

the priestess said, "Daisy was much more concerned about this Santeria spell. She told me she needed protection from an evil one. I cautioned Daisy that this was the more important altar of the two. I use many symbols here representing much powerful energy. Red peppers stuffed into a glass of pomegranate wine, bay leaves, animal horns, an image of Papa Legba, our intermediary and an amulet spell bottle filled with licorice, brown sugar and salt."

Jorge stopped Jean Baptiste, blurting out, "Daisy wore the same amulet necklace. It's among her personal effects at the HPD. I didn't know its significance till just now. Come to think of it, she also had a tiny red bag with three stones in it."

"Yes, my child," Jean Baptiste said, "I gave those to Daisy to keep with her at all times."

"Exactly who was Daisy so afraid of?" I excitedly asked.

Jean Baptiste handed me a large black skull candle from the altar. "I had Daisy etch his name backwards on the bottom," she explained. Jean Baptiste turned the candle upside down. *BILAS AFATSUM.*

"Son of a bitch!" I cried. "Mustafa Salib!"

Chapter Forty-Eight

The FBI's Cyber Crime Division in Washington D.C. had completed their
analysis on the computer seized at 1172 East 181 Street, Washington
Heights and came up with an address for Mustafa Salib at 63 Thompson
Street, New York City. NYPD's Joint Terrorist Task Force has been
staking out the building for a few days but Salib has not shown up. The
building looked uninhabitable; a construction crew was preparing to knock
it down. The FBI's Cyber Crime Division came up with another address for
Salib on East 12th Street in Manhattan. The task force hit the apartment an
hour ago. No arrests were made, but a large quantity of the deadly drug
fentanyl was found. It's a quick acting creation of synthetic opioid,
trafficked and packaged as heroin but it is fifty times as lethal. Accidental
contact of 5 or 6 grains of this material can kill you if inhaled or absorbed
through skin abrasions. Again, Salib's logo *Habibi,* in bright blue letters
was stamped on each small vial.

Arturo Colona sounded very agitated and wanted to talk to me about
something that he needed to get off his chest. We met in the Reptile House
in the Bronx Zoo on Fordham Road. While lizards, turtles, frogs and Cuban
Crocs idly occupied their cages, Arturo began spilling his guts. "Frank, can
we keep what I'm gonna say off the record?"

"Keep what off the record?" I asked.
Arturo, visibly shaken, said, "Please, what I'm about to tell you can't be
used against me. I need to know that."

"I'll do whatever I can to protect you, my friend," I replied. He thought for
a moment and said, "One day, Mustafa, Hani and I were partying all night
at Mustafa's apartment on Thompson Street, when two girls dropped in and
joined the party. The girls were snorting coke. They were laughing and
playing around with Hani and Mustafa. One of the girls, Daisy put some

music on and she and the other girl Felicity began to dance like strippers without a pole. They looked pros to me."

I almost shit when Arturo mentioned the girl's names. He has vital information that could lead to their killer. I didn't interrupt him and let him continue to talk.

"At one point, Hani and Daisy started to get it on in the bedroom. Salib grabbed Felicity by the wrists and tried to force his tongue down her throat. She pushed him off and spit on the floor. That was her swan song. He came at her. She ran to the door, but he grabbed her by the hair, overpowered her and threw her to the ground. He started to pull her pants off to screw her. In the struggle, she was able to grab her stiletto and slammed him across his face. Hearing the commotion, Daisy ran to help Felicity. The two girls were no match for Mustafa's strength. He brutally punched the girls in the face. Daisy was fiery. She struggled, jumping on his back, kicking him and screaming, fighting for her life. Mustafa flung Daisy across the room, like a fucking rag doll. That rag doll slammed up against the wall and slumped onto the floor. She was groaning from her injuries. Mustafa removed his belt and strangled the girl to death. Felicity was moaning and coming to. Again, she tried for the door. Hani hit her from behind and smashed her head on the floor till she was dead. Frank, these guys were no strangers to violence believe me. They took it in stride. There was absolutely nothing I could do. I feared that they would kill me. I still do."

His eyes began to well up. "Frank, you gotta believe me, I had nothing to do with it. I don't want to take the rap for this. I'll tell ya this, when the apartment in Washington Heights was raided, Mustafa was on the street watching the whole thing go down. Since the raid, he's moved his operation to Thompson Street in the East Village."

I thought I'd throw him a curve ball and said, "You mean the building they're knocking down?"

"You know about it?" he said.

Now I had the killers of Daisy and Felicity. I wanted him to think that I knew more about Mustafa than I did. "Yes, I know about the building. C'mon, keep talking."

Arturo, gazing down said, "Mustafa hated Daisy. He hated that Hani was fucking Daisy. Daisy and her cousin Felicity were terrified of Mustafa. They knew that he was evil and Daisy was trying to convince Hani to break ties with him. One day when Felicity and Mustafa were alone in Mustafa's apartment, Mustafa put his moves on Felicity. The young girl lost a tooth in the battle of the sexes and took a few kidney punches as well. When Daisy saw Felicity's bruises she freaked out and threatened to go to the cops. Ayman was able to calm her down, but in Mustafa's mind, he couldn't take any chances. This eventually sealed the girl's fate. Sooner or later, Mustafa was going to kill them. He and Mustafa gave them free coke and they kept coming back regardless of any fear they had."

"Who dumped their bodies in Harrison?" I asked.

"Uh…It was me and Mustafa. Frank, I had no choice. I didn't want to end up dead. Believe me, I had nothing to do with killing them."
"Frank, there's something else I gotta get off my chest. Mustafa is planning something big in New York. I only heard bits and pieces about killing a lot of people. I don't know when or where it's gonna happen."

"Lemme ask ya Arturo, have you heard of Anna Zharkov?"

His face was blank and he went into a silent mode. I shoved my finger into his chest to wake him up. "Arturo you know this is important. People are gonna die. Do you know Zharkov?"

"Frank, I'm not in Salib's inner circle. I heard him mention her name, but I never met her."

My voice heated as I snapped, "Well you'd better get closer to him, if you don't want a murder rap hanging over your head!"

I left the Zoo, I told Arturo to wait thirty minutes to leave, just to be safe. He shouldn't be seen with me for obvious reasons. I drove a few blocks over to Little Italy, Arthur Avenue, in the Bronx. I stopped at Joe Pappalardo's restaurant for a bite to eat. Fried rice balls stuffed with Asiago cheese, coupled with a nice glass of red wine. It doesn't get any better than that.

Later the next day I called Arturo's cell phone. A female answered. She said that Arturo was rushed to the emergency room at St. Vincent's Hospital in New York City. He died at 2:04 p.m.

"Who are you?" I asked.

"Ebony Hamilton," she replied. "Arturo's girlfriend."

When Arturo was admitted to the hospital, his girlfriend was with him. I wanted to find out more about Arturo's sudden death. I paid Ebony a surprise visit at her pre-war apartment building in Harlem. A gaunt black woman, in her mid-twenties answered the door of the 3rd floor walk up.

"Ebony Hamilton?" I asked.

"Yeah," she said, "who wants to know?"

I identified myself and asked if we could talk for a few minutes.

Reluctantly she let me in. "C'mon in detective, sit yourself down."

Ebony looks like she's seen better days. I'm sure she's been sampling Arturo's drugs. The sparsely furnished apartment looked unloved just like her.

"You want a drink?" Ebony asked bleary eyed as she poured a glass of vodka.

"No thanks," I replied.

She smiled, guzzled the vodka down and said, "It's five o'clock somewhere baby."

"Not here," I chuckled. "It's noon here."

"Not in Harlem detective," she remarked. "It's always midnight here."
"I understand Arturo died from something he ate that he was allergic to. Is that correct?" I asked.

"So the docs say Detective Frank. Ya know, Arturo did have an allergy to peanuts. He was careful not to eat them."

"Ebony, tell me what happened," I asked.

"Well, me and my man had something to eat at Miss Browns Cafeteria on West 122nd Street. Ya know it's self serve but Miss Brown makes all the food and lists the ingredients on the display signs. A few minutes after Arturo bit into one of the cookies, he had trouble breathing. He was grabbing at his throat. He was turning blue and collapsed on the floor. I managed to grab his needle in his pocket."

"You mean an Epi-Pen?" I asked.

"Yeah, whatever. Arturo always carried it. He never went anywhere without it. It was his life line," she said.

Ebony sighed, "I tried to use it to save him but it had nothing in it. It was empty. All's I know is it wouldn't work. Somebody musta called 911 and you know the rest of the story. It was too late for my baby."

"How long did you know Arturo?" I asked. Ebony's forehead was sweating profusely. She poured herself another vodka. That visibly steadied her.

"About five years," she answered. "Is there anything else?" she asked. "If not I gotta go to a teachers appointment at my son's school."

"Nothing else," I replied. "Thanks for your time. Once again, sorry for you loss."

Something wasn't right. Something was off about her demeanor. She didn't seem to be too upset about Arturo's untimely death. Instinctively I waited outside Ebony's dilapidated apartment building for a while just to see if she was telling me the truth about the teachers meeting.

At 3:00 p.m. She left her building and drove her banged up jalopy away. At a safe distance, I followed her to her destination, a destination I'm very familiar with. You got it, Enrico's Bar. Is it coincidental that Ebony takes a ride to the same bar where I picked up my hit man for hire money? All roads lead to an Arab connection. Ebony emerged from Enrico's with a gym bag. I left there with a package and now she is as well. Will wonders never cease!

I tailed her back to Harlem where she paid visits to several retailers like Carols Daughter and Harlem Chic, two of Harlem's upscale shops. Ebony could hardly manage all the shopping bags she carried. Her last stop was to the Payless shoe store before heading back to her apartment. So much for the teachers meeting, there was more here than meets the eye. Ebony will be seeing me again soon and an expensive shopping spree won't be on our agenda.

Chapter Forty-Nine

Hamilton is a scofflaw. Her driver's license has been revoked, has no car insurance and owes hundreds of dollars in unpaid parking tickets, which she blatantly ignores and just goes on her merry way. Ebony Hamilton is a scofflaw!

I contacted her and asked her to come in to the office for a few more questions about Arturo's death. I was surprised she agreed to come in. Tyra and I questioned her in our interview room. First, I read Ebony her Miranda Rights; my opening hand was pretty strong, two aces in the hole.

"Ebony," I said, "I've done a little due diligence on you and discovered that you are in violation of section 511 of the New York State Vehicle and Traffic Law, aggravated unlicensed operation of a motor vehicle."

"Say what?" she said, "I ain't done anythin' aggravated."
"Your license was revoked last year," Tyra said, "You are in debt to the city to the tune of $1,957 in unpaid parking tickets."

"In addition," I said, "you continue to drive an uninsured vehicle. We have impounded your Ford, the one you just parked downstairs in the parking garage. You're guilty of a misdemeanor or two."

"You can't do that!" she squawked defiantly.

"Oh yes we can and we did!" Tyra shouted, "more bad news, we're gonna detain you here for a bit. We'll make you nice and comfortable, don't worry, my dear!"

"What do you people want from me?" Ebony pleaded, "I ain't done nothin' wrong."

"We'll be the judge of that," I said.

She was held overnight in a holding cell to give her time to ponder her predicament.

We let her stew as long as was allowed by law. After two days we re-interviewed Ebony about the day Arturo died. You don't have to be Albert Einstein to figure out that's the real reason we had her in our grasp in the first place. She again insisted that she'd done nothing wrong and didn't need an attorney.

She chain smoked while we interrogated her. "Ebony, we're trying to help you out," I said. "Don't be your own worst enemy. Tell us what happened to Arturo Colona. What really happened?"

"Ebony, we know all about your trip to Enrico's Bar and your shopping spree the day I knocked on your door," I said. "It tells us a lot about you and the situation, if you know what I mean. We also know Enrico's is a drop for payoff money for people who have done or are about to do a job for some unsavory characters, possibly Arabs."

It was easy to see she was in no condition to withstand our hard-line interrogation. She was suffering from alcohol withdrawal and was trembling and nauseous. Her weakened state was to our advantage and we knew it.

"I gotta get a drink," she bellowed. "I gotta get outta here now. I'm sick. I'm 26-years old. I can't spend any time locked up," she bemoaned.

Ebony began sobbing uncontrollably. "Help me. Please."

"Ebony, we can't help you till you help yourself," Tyra said.

"What'd ya mean?" Ebony cried.

"I'm gonna show you some photos of men you may or may not recognize," I said, "Just nod if you recognize one."

I held up five pictures, Mustafa Salib and four others got no response. The 6th one, Ayman Hani got a timid nod from Ebony.

"You know this man?" Tyra asked.

Ebony was inconsolable. "That's him," she barked, "He told me to slip the nut cookie to Arturo and to make the Epi-Pen break. He said he'd kill me and my son if I didn't do it. I'm sorry Arturo, I'm so, so sorry," she cried. "I had no choice. I'm not a killer. I was scared. My baby Rashad is only 7-years old."

Rashad was already in the safekeeping of his grandmother and will remain there for the long haul. Ebony will have to do time. How much will depend on the court.

Arturo Colona can never testify against Hani and Salib for the "West Street Murders." The psychopaths made sure of that.

Chapter Fifty

The next day we were going to execute a search warrant for Salib's basement apartment on Thompson Street, NYC. I don't have to tell you we'd hope to catch him in his apartment with his pants down. The raiding party consisted of me, Rich, Ace, Tyra, and Jorge. We all had a piece of this thing and I'm sure we wanted to see Salib and Hani in handcuffs. Personally, I wanted to keep it simple. I didn't want the grandiose parade of EMS vehicles and armored personnel carriers assisting in executing the warrant. We were plenty of talent to get the job done.

The "A" team all rode together in a black van to Mustafa's apartment. Our Kevlar flak jackets had pouches housing armor plates, which boost the gear's bullet mitigating powers. We wore our raid jackets over the flaks to identify ourselves as police officers.

On the ride over, no one said a word. As we pulled up to the curb, a wrecking ball was slamming into the seventh floor of the building, knocking chunks of the brick façade, cement and steel girders to the ground. Parts of the building were being demolished. An excavator was scooping up the debris and placing it in a large dumpster in the middle of the courtyard.

We collected ourselves for a few minutes, preparing to get the show on the road. A quick prayer was said, and we headed out. Over by the far end of the building we noticed a large muscular African American, in his early forties, wearing a protective helmet and dressed in brown overalls. He looked to be in charge, shouting out orders to the steam shovel operator and a few laborers who were picking up pieces of debris.

My brother was the first to sound off. "Hey, let's get going and see what the guy in charge has to say before we hit the door."

The foreman had a twenty mission stare on his face when we walked up to him wearing our raid jackets with the word police imprinted across the front and back. His eyes lit up as Jorge, whose shield hung down from a chain around his neck identified himself and said in an abrasive tone, "Police, who you are?"

"Al Connors, the foreman."

He appeared extremely nervous and asked, "Uh, what can I do for you?"

My brother barked, "Yo, we got a search warrant for the basement apartment."

Rattled, the foreman muttered, "Uh, the building is condemned. You see we're, uh, knocking it down. Most of the building has been vacated."

Ace showed him photos of Salib and Anna Zharkov and said, "Have you seen them around?"

The foreman, Al Connors, shrugged his shoulders and replied, "The guy just left with another guy. I don't know the woman. What's this all about?"

Ace replied, "Police business."

I presented Al with the search warrant. "Now," I said, "we could knock the door down, or we could do it the easy way and you could unlock it for us."

Al handed us the master key. Tyra got Al's attention and said, "Al, no phone calls. Ya understand?" He shook his head yes, pointing to a door to the left of the main entrance of the building. "Through that door, the last apartment on the left," he said.

We entered the basement door with our guns out. Tyra raised her weapon, as I pointed my shotgun at the middle of the metal door. Jorge slid the key into the lock, turning it slowly and unlocking the door. Ace shoved the door open and we rushed in shouting "Police!" No one was home. Jorge stood guard outside of the apartment. The electricity hadn't been turned off in the apartment. Tyra flipped on the lights and we began to systematically secure each room. We felt the tremors of the wrecking ball hitting the floors above us. Clusters of water bugs and cockroaches descended into the basement apartment. Nonetheless, we had to stay focused on the job at hand. We confiscated some papers written in Arabic and two laptops.

My brother and I were noising around in the bedroom and discovered a third laptop under the bed. These could hopefully yield plenty of intelligence. We found a bloody rag under the kitchen sink. Perhaps, it would be Daisy or Felicity's DNA.

Jorge hurried into the apartment and signaled that someone was coming. We took positions on either side of the door. The key turned in the lock. The door opened and the man himself, the elusive Ayman Hani walked in. "Freeze motherfucker," I yelled.

Hani didn't go down easy. He put up a ferocious fight, but we managed to get him cuffed. The big bad wolf shit his pants in fear. Enough said.

"Remember me?" I shouted.

"Yeah," he said scowling. "I shoulda killed you when I had the fucking chance."

"You're under arrest for the murders of Daisy Soto and Felicity Dominquez. You have the right to remain silent," I read him his Miranda Rights. "You scum suckers are planning a sarin attack, huh!"

Rich grabbed Hani by the shoulder and spun him around. "Where are Mustafa and Anna Zharkov, you piece of shit?"

Hani dropped his head. Richie screamed, "Look at me scumbag!"

Hani looked us dead in the eye and said, "I want a lawyer."

We had finished our forensic sweep of the place. Jorge found blood spatter behind a large mirror leaning on a living room wall and lots more on the bathroom walls and tub. There was a stain that suspiciously looked like dried blood on the carpet. We cut the patch out and took it to be tested for DNA evidence. Tyra was astute enough to notice a few tiny drops of dried blood on Hani's sneakers. The size 12 sneakers were bagged as well and placed into evidence. The DNA findings hopefully will contribute to seal the fate of Ayman Hani and Mustafa Salib for the murders of Daisy and Felicity.

Chapter Fifty-One

Mike's phone kept ringing and then went directly to voice mail. I left a clear message that he'd definitely understand. "Mike, I got your fuckin' cousin. He's in custody. We've got a huge amount of evidence mounting against him. Call me."

It wasn't ten minutes before he called. Mike asked where his cousin was being held and if he was cooperating. "He's lawyered up, Mike; he's no fool, he's been around the block a few times."

Mike sounded relieved. "Okay Frankie, thanks. I'll be in touch."

Captain Matthews texted me for an ASAP meeting. Tyra, Angel and I quickly convened in his office. "I was just notified that Ayman Hani hung himself in his jail cell this morning," C. J. Matthews said.

"Son of a bitch, shit!" we said in unison.

"Farid Mahadi paid him a visit this morning before his arraignment," Matthews said, "he's the Imam of the As-Jami in Manhattan's financial district. That mosque keeps showing up on our radar. Law enforcement has an undercover cop in the mosque, trying to get a handle on what's going on."

Matthews continued, "FBI Special Agent Ken Spencer finally provided us with the dossier on Salib." He began to read from their report. "His vital stats are: Salib was raised in the Syrian Desert by his paternal grandfather Usman Salib, after the death of Mustafa's parents. His vital stats are, age 46, height 6 feet 5 inches, slender build, full beard and mustache, single, no children. Educated as a chemist at Kings College in London. There are reports that Usman, in addition to being a master bomb maker, was an alleged pedophile who victimized his own flesh and blood grandson,

Mustafa beginning at an early age. By the time Mustafa was sixteen years old, he couldn't tolerate his grandfathers' sexual abuse any longer. That year he snuck into Usman's tent, beheaded and castrated the old man. He displayed these trophies on sticks for all in the camp to see. From then on, Mustafa was feared by all."

"He's a fuckin' animal!" I blurted out.
"Reliable intel has turned up a threat of an immense sarin gas attack on a New York City mall," Matthews went on to say. "Mall security is being amped up. Bomb sniffing dogs and extra personnel are being assigned to secure the malls until Salib is apprehended, dead or alive."

"Looks like we have our work cut out for us Captain," Tyra said.

"Sure looks like it," C.J. said.

After the meeting, I called Mike to tell him Hani was dead. He appeared happy and sad all at once. "He was my cousin, but he was a bad seed," Mike said. "I was afraid of him. I don't think he could face anymore jail time. He told me he would rather kill himself than go back inside those walls."

Truer words were never spoken.

Chapter Fifty-Two

Cindy Galgano texted and asked me to meet her at the Oyster Bar in Grand Central Terminal. She said it was urgent.

When I arrived, Cindy was sipping on a martini. Her eyes were puffy and swollen. "Frankie," she said, "I'm so glad you're here."

"Are you okay Cindy?" I asked, "You look like you've been crying."

Cindy began to sob. "My father died last night, he had a massive heart attack. Oh Frankie, I don't know what I'll do without him." She covered her face with both hands and continued to cry.

"Cindy, I'm so sorry for your loss." Meanwhile I was thinking that my chances of getting wacked had diminished greatly. The guy who most wants me dead, is dead.

"I'm here to make things right," she said, "I went to my father's apartment this morning. I was trying to get his affairs in order and find a suit to bury him in. I came across a small safe hidden in his closet. One of the keys on his key ring opened it. It contained a copy of his will and some of my mother's jewelry. There was also a DVD in the safe. I'm handing it over to you. I watched it this morning."

"What's on the disc?" I exclaimed.

"I rather you watch it and then we'll talk," she replied.
"Does Mike know about any of this?" I asked.

"No," she cried, "and that's the way I want to keep it."

My curiosity was killing me. I rushed back to my office and viewed the DVD alone. The footage captured Chief Larry Christopher meeting with Nick Galgano. Whoa! The audio quality was poor, but the images were crystal clear. Here was the mole. Larry was taking money from Nick. Nick and Larry toasted each other with some wine, "Here's to a long and prosperous future," Nick said. "25k, to start and there will be more where that came from," Galgano laughed.

"Hey we each have something the other needs," Larry toasted.

My next step was to bring the disc directly to Hogan and Beau to view. They viewed it in astonishment.

"Arrest the chief immediately!" Hogan said curtly.

When Hogan, Beau Winslow and I walked into Larry's office, we found him slumped over his desk. John Hogan tried to rouse him without success. 911 was called and Larry was rushed to White Plains Hospital where he was admitted. After running a battery of tests, it was determined that Larry was abusing oxycodone and had overdosed. Hogan assigned two detectives, 24/7, to monitor his hospital room.

The doctors permitted us to see him the next morning when he was lucid. The DA, Beau, I and our videographer were on hand. I formally placed Larry under arrest and read him his rights. Larry was physically weak, but piped up and said with a look of shock, "Arrested? For what!"

John Hogan informed Larry about Galgano's video tucked away in evidence.

"That rat prick! He set me up!" Larry muttered.

"Larry, that's all in the past," Hogan said. "Galgano kicked the proverbial bucket last night."

"Yes, Larry," I said, "Nick's daughter discovered the video hidden among his personal effects."

Christopher broke down weeping.

"What happened to you Larry?" Beau asked. "You have sold your badge and compromised our entire office and everyone in it. How did we end up here?"

"You are complicit with every move Nick made using information you provided him." Hogan chided him.

Larry took a breath and sighed. "C'mon Larry fess up," I yelled. "Why did you betray your badge?"

"You want to know how I got in this position," Larry said as he lifted his head. "Here's how," Larry sobbed. "I started taking pain killers for the back injury I got skiing . The doctor had no problem with keeping me medicated for a few months. At some point, the doctor cut me off, but it was too late. I was hooked, all the way. I felt that I would do anything, and I mean anything to get my hands on those pills. You can't imagine the desperation I felt. I couldn't believe it was happening to me. I made a connection through an old informant of mine and my habit got even worse. I think you've all witnessed the changes in me. I became weak and vulnerable; a pathetic excuse for a human being. I needed two things, money and pills. Nick Galgano had both. He was only too happy to work with me. Through his humiliation he continued, "Nick wanted you dead Frankie. He even made me call off your protection detail a few times so his goons would have a better shot at you. I'm sorry Frankie....so sorry. I know I'm finished."

"Anything more you want to get off your chest?" Beau asked.

"One day I walked in on Lizzie." Larry became choked up and had to stop for a minute. "She…was stealing some of my oxy pills. Of course I was outraged, but it didn't stop her. She got hooked too. She needed to go to into rehab. It's very expensive. The money I took was partly for her too. Once I lost my girl Lizzie, the walls came tumbling down. It's my fault she's dead."

"I think we're finished," Hogan said in disgust. "Larry, you've made your bed. You've not only disgraced this office, you're facing some pretty heavy jail time. Gentlemen, we're done here. Let's leave Larry alone with his betrayal."

Chapter Fifty-Three

Since intel confirmed that New York City malls were a potential sarin gas target, security was stepped up radically. Ace and I covered the Westfield World Trade Center Mall. The Westfield mall is a vibrant architectural wonder. Its' center piece is the Oculus designed by Spanish architect Santiago Calatrava to resemble a winged dove. It's a masterpiece.

We spotted a few FBI agents dressed in assault fatigues on patrol too. After several hours on foot patrol, we decided to get to the car and surveil the parking garage for a while to break the monotony. Suddenly, a woman ran by us. She was moving fast and was being chased by two agents, yelling, "Halt, FBI!" She ducked behind a car as Ace and I joined forces with the agents. Ace drove past the car where the woman was last seen. Nothing! We drove slowly around the area looking for her, but there was no sign of her. Then we spotted her about 200 feet away. "Is that Anna Zharkov?" I said excitedly.

"Sure looks like the photo that Interpol sent!" Ace said excitedly.

I yelled out, "Freeze Anna, you're under arrest!"

She stood her ground, drew a semi-automatic pistol, aimed it directly at us and began pumping bullets at us. The bitch shattered our windshield with the spray of bullets. I drew my 9mm and began to return fire. Anna began to run for cover, as Ace hit the accelerator pedal hard. Zero to sixty is a commonly used expression; Ace almost pushed the gas peddle through the floor. In an instant, we were on her. I literally could see the whites of her eyes. It was her. Anna. There was a dull thud when the car hit her and hurled her into mid-air over the four foot retaining wall of the parking structure. Ace hit the breaks hard, stopping inches before slamming into the protective wall. We leapt from the car and looked down over the wall. We had a birds eye view of what remained of Zharkov after she careening down nine stories to her death. Her head was split in two, like two halves of a melon. The FBI Agents caught up with us, just in time to see the gruesome scene below. Believe me, this is what nightmares are made of.

"She was in an off limits restricted area of the mall," one of the agents said. "We spotted her. She raised a weapon then began to run. We gave chase, you guys joined in."

"She was shooting directly at us," I said. "We ran her off the roof."

In a matter of minutes, cop cars surrounded Zharkov's body. A large crowd of onlookers gathered at the scene. Technicians from the M.E.'s Office soon arrived and proceeded to scrape all the body parts into a body bag and take her for her last joyride to their office for an autopsy. Her ID verified it was Anna Zharkov. Anna, according to some beliefs will now go to heaven and be the *Chief of the 70 virgins and the fairest of the fair.* Sounds to me like women get the short end of the stick on this one.

Zharkov was likely looking for a suitable location to place a sarin canister for the next attack; however her luck ran out today.

Chapter Fifty-Four

FBI agent Taj Taha was born in Amman Jordan during the reign of King Hussein's forty seven year monarchy. His father Rami was the chief editor of the Jordanian Times, the Kingdom's only English language daily newspaper. He graduated from Georgetown University in D.C. top of his class. Taj Taha was also working as an undercover agent in the As-Jami Mosque for the last year. Ace arranged to introduce me to Taj over lunch in his office.

"Taj, this is Detective Frank Santorsola," Ace said. "The three of us have a common goal, stop Mustafa Salib and anyone like him."
"I've heard a lot about you, Frank," Taj said.

"Likewise," I replied.

It was easy to see why Taj Taha could assimilate into the mosque crowd. He was medium height, dark, handsome and well spoken. He has a definite likeability factor and looked the part. He was a tremendous asset to the FBI's efforts in fighting terrorism.

He said, "I've finally managed to break down some barriers at the As-Jami Mosque. These people are very suspicious of strangers and extremely difficult to develop relationships with. Finally a few months ago, I managed to connect with a worshipper named Jari Reza. Jari is a bit of a loner who needed a friend and someone to vent to. I'm fulfilling that role. We both attend the Friday noon prayer services and then hang at his apartment in Chelsea, on West 23rd Street in Manhattan. We discuss world politics, music, women and Muslimism. Jari is a confirmed jihadist and believes that I am as well. He's agreed to involve me with the movement. He is from a very wealthy family in Lebanon.

"Taj, sounds like this could be pay dirt," I said, "What's next?"

"Jari has invited me to his house in Southampton this weekend. I gladly accepted his invitation. Who knows what's going on out there? I know its one step closer to the head of the snake," he said.

"Can we back you up in anyway, Taj?" Ace asked.

"No Sal, I have to work this as a lone wolf," he said. "The Bureau wants back-up but I refused. I can't afford to have even the slightest impropriety in the picture. I've got them by the balls and that's where I intend to keep them. Contact with you and my office needs to be at a bare minimum. I'm constantly tested to prove my veracity."
"As we say," he continued, "Ala Aini Wa Raasi. Translated, it means I will absolutely get it done."

"Be safe Taj," Ace said. We all shook hands and Taj left the room.

Chapter Fifty-Five

We didn't hear from Taj for several days. On Tuesday he asked to meet again at Ace's office on Hudson Street in lower Manhattan, to update us in on his undercover operation. What he did say was that he's met Mustafa Salib.

"After the Friday noon service at As-Jami Mosque," Taj explained, "Jari and I left the city and headed to Cobble Field Way in Southampton. Jari is renting an exquisite secluded house on a private beach overlooking the Atlantic Ocean. It sits on several acres in an off the beaten path location. There was a country barn on the property that I was not privy to," he continued. "Some of the other guests spent quite a bit of time in the barn, including Mustafa. I suspect it's some kind of workshop for these fanatics. I just couldn't get close to it," Taj said. "Apparently, privacy was a main concern for Jari. He proudly gave me the tour of the six bedroom, five bath perfectly maintained house."

The Southampton area is the playground for the rich and famous. One million dollars may buy you a fixer upper, handy man special.

"Friday afternoon was uneventful. Friday evening, the other invited nomads showed up. These were part of the hierarchy of the movement. Farid Mahadi, Imam of As-Jami Mosque was there among a group of six others, all devoted to their cause. We shared a meal. They all bantered and conversed back and forth like new friends do."

"Make no mistake," Taj said, "all of Jari's guests are like-minded jihadists. The conversation never veered far from the same topic, over and over again, in one form or another, bolstering terrorism and the inbred loathing of all infidels."

"Sounds like a fun crowd," I laughed.

"Of course, even this hard core bunch made exceptions to the rule when ordered to do so," Taj said.

"Exception to the rule? How so?" Ace asked.

"Camellia!" Taj revealed. "Mustafa Salib is a well respected and feared leader. Two weeks ago, he met an exotic Latina temptress. She is a Christian, in her early thirties, a beauty for the ages. The jihadists were ordered to keep their traps shut about Mustafa's pussy of choice," Taj chuckled. "If there was any dissent about Camellia, there would be hell to pay. Once Salib laid eyes on her, he fell hard and fast," Taj said, "He's in over his head in lust!"

"Taj, this is the best Intel we have so far, great work," I said.

"Were there any problems?" Ace asked. "Did everything run smoothly for you?"

"No problems, it went smooth as silk," Taj said. "Jari invited me back next weekend. I must have been a hit with them."

"By the way," Ace asked. "Did you pick up any information on the other attendees?"

"Guys, I don't have to tell you, my life is at stake here. I could only manage to capture a few images of the guests on my hidden camera device. I made copies for you two."

Taj laid out six images on Ace's desk. One I recognized as Farid Mahadi, the Imam. Another photo literally made my knees buckle. It was like being hit over the head with a two- by- four. It was of a very familiar face. A face I knew and placed my respect and trust in for several years. It was of a person who professed his undying loyalty to me. The face of a person, who at times had my very life in his hands. The face of Mike Baraka.

"Taj, Ace," I yelled, waving the picture wildly in the air, "this is Mike Baraka!"

"You're fucking kidding me, Cheech!" Ace replied.

"Fuck, I kid you not!" I ranted in disbelief.

"Someone you know?" Taj asked.

"Damn right .1" I replied. "Someone that I treated like a brother. Someone I saved from doing ten years in federal prison."

Taj stood there, shaking his head. He didn't know what to say.

"Okay gentlemen," Ace said, as he stood behind his desk, "let's get to work on the mother of all fucking covert missions. *Operation Kismet.*"
"Let's put these assholes in Guantanamo Bay, where they belong," I said.

Chapter Fifty-Six

I'd say it was time to pop the big question to Denise and make it official. I wanted to propose to Denise in the most romantic place in New York City. Nothing better than the St. Cloud Rooftop at the Knickerbocker Hotel in Times Square. The mansard style roof encompasses a 3800-square-foot Sky Pod of the most the prime NYC air space. I rented the corner open air pod which really puts you on cloud nine. The rooftop itself is sixteen stories above the *Crossroads of the World.* The Beaux-Arts style 600 square feet pod offers swoon-able visual chatter of the Times Square LEDs and live streaming billboards. The terrace is dwarfed on all sides by towering right angle office spaces and the iconic Paramount's *time is a money* ticking clock situated under the Times Square Waterford Crystal Ball. It is framed by twenty fabulous copper-green, 2- feet high lion heads sitting atop its protective walls. The views of Times Square are unparalleled.

First I had to spend the afternoon on Friday picking out her engagement ring. DA John Hogan recommended Hakin Jewelers in Manhattan's Diamond District. Hakins' was owned and operated by a family of Hasidic Jews who've been dealing in precious stones for over 70 years.

Two men sporting full length beards and yarmulkes on their heads greeted me from behind the counter after they buzzed me in. Dressed in black slacks and white shirts with rolled up sleeves, they were ready to show me diamonds.

I introduced myself to the older one.

"I'm Abraham Hakin, call me Abe. This is my grandson, Moishe. How can I help you Frank?"

"The DA, John Hogan recommended Hakins' to me," I said.

"Oh, the Hogan's are good customers of mine," Abe replied. "Our families have been doing business together for decades. Wonderful people."

"Now, what did you have in mind?" Abe asked.

I discussed my budget with him and he gave me a short education on diamonds, shape, clarity, the whole ball of wax. We settled on a gorgeous round stone in a simple raised setting. It was as brilliant as the sun. Perfect!

The next day, Saturday, Denise and I drove into Manhattan and strolled around the city to take in a few sights. We stopped into Pete's Tavern in Gramercy Park. It's one of the oldest Pub's in New York City, serving customers since the late 1800's. The famous writer O. Henry was a frequent visitor.

Our hostess, Alyx-Rae, had a thick Irish brogue. Denise asked, "What county in Ireland are you from?"

Alyx-Rae proudly beamed and replied, "County Armagh. What can I get for you?"

"What beer is on tap?" I asked.

"Guinness, Harp, Kilkenny and Murphy's Irish Red," Alyx-Rae replied.

Denise replied, "I'll have a Guinness."

"Make that two," I said.

"I love it here Frank," Denise said, while she marveled at the old world pub.

"I'm starving," Denise said, looking over the menu. "I'll have the Shepherd's Pie."

"I'll have the Bangers and Mash," I said.
Our lives have been so chaotic lately, we felt normal just sitting here together hand in hand. It's really the simple things in life that count.

After a wonderful lunch, we strolled through the Chelsea Market.

"I have a little surprise for you, Denise!" I said as we walked.

"Surprise?" she said grinning, "I love surprises. What is it?"

"Let's go, I'll show you, we'll have to cab it," I said smiling.

We took a cab to Times Square and arrived at the Knickerbocker Hotel. Denise looked like a little girl on Christmas morning, full of excitement. "Frankie, what's going on?" she exclaimed.

"We're gonna be overnight guests here!" I replied. "I think we deserve a break, don't you?"

"Yes, we do," she said eagerly.

The hotel had just undergone a major renovation, every detail was perfect. We gawked like two kids in a candy store and took it all in. We passed the doormen, who were wearing black bowler hats and double-breasted tail jackets.

I had packed a small bag that held enough stuff for Denise and I to manage an overnighter.

The bellman showed us to our room on the 12th floor. "Oh Frankie, this is perfect," Denise said grinning. "Let's try out the bed."

"You read my mind," I replied.

We made love passionately until we both were too tired to continue. We dozed off for thirty minutes. We quickly showered and dressed for dinner.

"Where are we going to eat?" Denise asked. "Is that a surprise too?"

"Yes it is, darling," I replied.

At 8:00 p.m., we took the elevator up to the 16th floor rooftop. "Do you like it?" I asked as we walked out to the out door space as Denise viewed the Times Square sky-line. The hostess showed us to our very own coveted nook in a 600 square feet Sky Pod.

"What do you think?" I asked as we both looked up at the Times Square skyscrapers all lit up.

"This is a spectacular place!" she said in wonderment, "I love it and you." We were seated on one of the long beige sofas and ordered some appetizers of assorted cheeses, olives, crackers and a bottle of Dom Perignon Champagne. We toasted each other. The Sky Pod can hold up to twenty five people, but it felt just perfect for the two of us.

In amazement she said, "This is the most beautiful view of New York I've ever seen. Thanks for taking me here. There's really nothing like this anywhere."

I reached into my pocket, got down on one knee and said, "Denise MacKenzie, my life was empty before I met you. You've made my life complete. Will you marry me?" Simultaneously, I flipped open the lid on the jewelry box to offer her the engagement ring.

"Will I marry you?" she roared, "Frankie, of course I'll marry you. I'm stunned. I'm thrilled! I'm gonna be your wife!"

Tears of joy streamed down her gorgeous face. She extended her left hand and I sealed the engagement by putting the ring on her ring finger. We kissed each other softly and exchanged whispers of deep love for one another. This was truly a night to remember.

"Frankie, thank you for the most perfect day of my life." Her tears were replaced by a loving smile.

I signaled the pianist and by prearranged request, she played, *Through the Fire*. The perfect finish to the perfect engagement to the perfect woman I love.

Chapter Fifty-Seven

On Friday, Taj was taking that trip out to the Hamptons. The only difference this week is that there will be a compliment of cops on hand to assist in *Operation Kismet.*

We have a moral obligation to society to take these animals off the street. Taj was wearing a state of the art eavesdropping device to record everything that went down. He was determined to get a glimpse into the barn. If it contained what we suspected, we could tie everything up in one neat big beautiful bow.

At 2:00 p.m. part of the A team positioned themselves a safe distance from the main house. Jari and Taj arrived at Cobble Field Way about 3:00 p.m. It was a cloudy cold day. The waves were crashing hard on the beach. Ace and I decided to surveil the house from Ace's Monterey Sports Yacht *The Ace of Spades* that he docked in nearby Montauk, Long Island. The boat provided us with an incredible vantage point, at the same time, as not being detected. We all were in radio contact and could hear Taj's wired conversations.

7:00 p.m. the house was filling up with guests. Our high-tech night vision binoculars gave us a great opportunity to hawk-eye the entire event. The house had loads of large windows, so visibility was good. The audio was on target as well. *Operation Kismet* was in full throttle.

After some friendly conversation, some of their conversation in their native language, the guests settled in for dinner in the dining room, where they continued their rhetoric, mostly about bringing every Muslim under Sharia Law. After dinner they all proceeded to the living room. There was a knock at the front door. Jari answered it. Three new visitors arrived.

It was the man himself, in the flesh, Mustafa Salib, all 6 feet 5 inches of him. Ace and I remained silent as we continued to focus our binoculars at the elusive figure and listen to any audio we could pick up.

Mustafa's arm candy was a show stopper. It must be Camellia hanging all over him. We heard Jari introduce "Taj Maloof", his undercover name, to Mustafa and Camellia. The third party reached his hand out to Taj and said, "Hello, I'm Mike, we met here last week."

Fucking Baraka, my head was spinning. He's travelling with the kingpin himself. Mustafa spoke briefly to the men, "Saturday morning we reconvene in the barn. Now I have some serious business to attend to. Allah Akbar, my brothers."

"Mustafa, come with me to the kitchen," Jari said, "I'll get you three some food and water after your journey. Follow me."

Taj took that opportunity to excuse himself. As we later discovered, Taj dashed up the back stairs to his bedroom. It was adjoining the master suite where Mustafa was staying. Taj's had a bag of tricks that contained a small alarm clock that doubled as a highly sensitive motion activated audio-video web cam. He secretly planted it on the dresser in Mustafa's bedroom. He escaped undetected. Perhaps, other than porn, it would capture some useful intelligence. Taj seized the opportunity to scope out the barn while Jari was hosting Salib, Camellia and Mike.

As the party continued inside, we could see Taj under the cover of evening, run quickly over to the barn. There was a ladder lying nearby, he rested it on the side of the barn and climbed it to peer into the window. He used a small high powered flashlight to view the darkened barn. He gave a thumbs up and said, "The barn is filled with several barrels of malathion, as well as canisters and what looks like bomb making components."

Taj, removed the ladder and once more sprinted back into the house. At that moment, a violent thunderstorm rocked the area. We could still hear Taj's transmissions, but he was breaking up badly. *The Ace of Spades* was bouncing all over the Atlantic. We all waited impatiently for about thirty minutes for Taj's signal to storm the place, as the wind and rain slammed through Cobble Field Way. Finally, Taj gave the signal we had been waiting for and shouted, "Kismet! Operation Kismet is in full throttle!"

Ace headed the boat for shore, as the FBI and the A team took the front and rear doors down. Ace tied up his boat at the pier at the back of the house and we ran into the chaos. Two of the suspected terrorists drew their weapons and began firing at cops. The threat was quickly neutralized. The rest of the bad guys surrendered. Tyra, Richie, Angel and Jorge were handcuffing them as Ace and I walked into the living room. I was looking for Mustafa, but I didn't see him. Taj motioned for Ace and me to follow him upstairs. "He's upstairs in the bedroom, he's got a girl with him," Taj said. We assumed Mustafa would be heavily armed so we proceeded cautiously up the stairs to the landing.

I kicked the door lock in and broke the door open. The three of us rushed in, armed and ready, took secure positions in the room. Our eyes immediately settled on a blood soaked bed. There was Mustafa, stark naked, handcuffed and shackled to the bed, his eyes glazed over, blood was spurting out of his wounds. He had three daggers imbedded in his upper torso. He was dead. What the fuck, I thought. Once again I was mystified. Who did us this favor?

The house was finally secured and all the suspects were under arrest. The grounds were now swarming with cop cars and more FBI agents than you could count. Helicopters hovered over the estate. Mike Baraka was among those taken into custody.

As the bomb squad dealt with securing the bomb making materials in the barn, CSI investigators did their thing in Mustafa's death room. His lifeless body was put in a body bag, zipped up and removed without any fanfare. The *Alhadi*, or leader, was off to the M.E.'s office. "Mustafa, go to the light, you evil piece of shit," I muttered. As everyone was leaving the bedroom, Taj asked me and Ace to stay for a moment. He picked up the alarm clock he'd placed on the dresser earlier. "I think I managed to get it all on video, from the beginning to end," Taj said smiling. He played the footage for the first time. The three of us anxiously viewed the footage.

Mustafa wasted no time in groping Camellia and throwing her down on the bed. He pounced on her and was clumsily trying to undress her. "Wait, my love," she said, "please don't rush, we have all night and I want to caress you from head to toe. But first, let's celebrate our love with some champagne."

Mustafa rolled over and Camellia got up and popped open the Armand de Brignac champagne that Jari provided.

"There it is," Taj yells, "she slips something into his drink." We had an unobstructed view of Camellia pouring a clear liquid into Mustafa's drink. She made sure that Mustafa had no such view. Camellia began to seductively dance over to the bed and the two made a lovers toast. She continued to gyrate like a veteran belly dancer as she removed her bra and thong. They toasted once again and drained their glasses dry.

"I have a little gift for you Mustafa," Camellia said.

"What is it?" Mustafa asked slurring slightly.

"I know you're gonna like these baby," Camellia said.

She pulled out a set of handcuffs. A drugged Mustafa grins. The spiked drink had taken effect. He looks disoriented. Camellia locks the handcuffs on his wrists and latches them to the slats on the headboard. He is now mumbling incoherently.

"I have a few more presents for you mi amore," Camellia said, as she danced around him and smiled. "But they are not from me. They were sent to you by Esteban Camacho!" Camellia shouts. She used Mustafa's belt to tie his feet.

"Whoa? Who the ....?" Salib murmurs. "Who the fuck is Esteban Camacho?" Salib babbles.

"How can you forget?" Camellia says. "He is the grandfather to Daisy Soto and Felicity Dominquez; the great grandpapa to Daisy's unborn boy. Remember, the girls you killed? Esteban Camacho's son is a Capo in the Puerto Rican mafia. They hired me to deliver the gifts to you. They requested that I look into your eyes as I deliver them. Mustafa, you messed with the wrong old man. The Camachos believe that revenge is sweet. Do you really think we met by accident? No mi corazon, it was all an elaborate plan and you fell for it, hook line and sinker. Do you think I'd get close to an ugly monster like you? Never!"

Mustafa's face became frozen in anger. Terror took over Salib. Mustafa groaned, "You sharmuta, I'll kill you!"

Camellia threw her head back and laughed. "I'll be long gone when they find your dead, rancid body rotting here."

Camellia reached for her bag and removed three razor edged daggers. She straddled Mustafa's limp body.

"The first gift is for Daisy," Camellia said, as she plunged the first dagger deep into his gut and twisted it.

Mustafa writhed and moaned in agony.

"The second gift is for Felicity," Camellia hissed. She stuck the second dagger into his chest and twisted it. He was barely moving now.

"The third gift is for the little one, Esteban's unborn grandson" She plunged the third dagger into his heart and twisted it. Gurgling sounds were heard from Mustafa but he appeared dead. Camellia un-straddled Mustafa and donned a floor length flowing black velvet hooded cape, slipped out of the window and disappeared into the night.

Chapter Fifty-Eight

The morning after the execution of *Operation Kismet,* DA Hogan held a meeting in his conference room. About twenty five people were in attendance. Anyone who worked on the investigation was included. FBI agent Taj Taha made a special guest appearance to assist with the wrap-up, as did Ace Lifrieri and Jorge Feliciano.

DA Hogan opened up the meeting. "Good morning, as you all know, Operation Kismet was executed last night. The success of this mission will go down in the annals of this office as one of the most memorable and well organized in our history. Each and every face I'm looking at should be proud to be part of this major takedown of Islamic terrorists. FBI Special Agent Taj Taha, HPD Detective Jorge Feliciano, NYPD Detective Sal Lifrieri, Detective Sergeant Tyra Williams, and Special Agent Rich Santorsola from the NEW York State Organized Crime Task Force have graced us with their presence this morning. A big thanks to you all. Your talents and determination helped enormously in the success of this mission. Oh, and let's not forget Joe Nulligan. He was severely injured at the on-set of this investigation."

A burst of applause filled the room.

Hogan continued, "As for all the dedicated law enforcement people in this room, each and every phone call, report, meeting and discussion were an integral part of the powerful mosaic that stopped the animals we arrested last night."

There was another burst of applause interrupting Hogan.

"Frank, Tyra, Rich and Jorge risked their lives, up close and personal," Hogan said. "Their style of policing led to the ultimate win. I can't thank them enough."

Another eruption of spontaneous applause rang out, this time combined with a standing ovation from everyone in the room. "I want the "A" team to take a few days off, that's an order," Hogan said. "But first I'd like you all to join me at the press conference at noon. Meeting adjourned."

"One thing I need to do," I said to Richie, "is to have a heart to heart with Mike Baraka at MCC." (Metropolitan Correctional Center 150 Park Row, NYC) "He needs to answer some questions."

"Frankie let's say our goodbyes for now," Taj said. "It's been a blast."

Taj and I shook hands. We both knew we had formed a lasting bond.

"I hope we're gonna have the chance to work again soon, Taj," I said, "That's if my heart can take it." I chuckled as I gestured to my heart.

"Frankie let's work and play together!" Taj said. "I could use a forth in a charity golf outing next Tuesday at Winged Foot Golf Club in Mamaroneck, NY. Tee off at 9:00 a.m. Are you interested?" Taj asked.

"I'll be there at 8:00 a.m. Sounds like a plan," I replied. "Meet you in the locker room."

"By the way," Taj said. "DA Hogan and NYPD Commissioner Rad Cooper will be in our foursome."

"Wow! Wonderful!" I remarked. "See you there."

Chapter Fifty-Nine

I met with Mike Baraka at the Metropolitan Correction Center on Park Row. As I entered the dismal holding cell, Mike was sitting on his bed. He didn't make eye contact with me.

"Mike, what the fuck happened to you?" I barked.

Mike growled! "What do you wanna know?"

"Mike," I yelled, "a fucking terrorist! After all we've been through, you fucking betrayed me!" My profane tirade continued. "After I put my life and career on the line for you, you betray me!! Why, why? I wanna know! What hold do they have on you?! You owe me an explanation!!"
"Listen Frank," he grumbled, "so many things happened. An explanation won't do much good anyway."

"Give it a try Mike," I demanded, "you fucking owe me that."

"After I got falsely arrested years ago," he said, "the world kinda crumbled under my feet. I felt like I had no solid ground. No foundation. I realized how flawed the system is."

"No solid ground?" I yelled. "The only fucking solid ground you woulda had was the floor of a 10 x 10 jail cell for ten years. I saved your ass. What kind of an excuse for a man are you?"

Mike looked me straight in the eye and said, "Remember when I traveled back to Jordan two years ago? I stayed in the Middle East for two months with my cousins Faisal and Hamzah. They took me all over the Middle East. There is nothing but poverty and bombed out buildings, especially in Syria and Iraq. The men sit around all day smoking cigarettes and talking politics. They have lost hope of any peace or prosperity in their lives or the lives of their children. My cousin Faisal took me to a camp in the ISIS caliphate in Northern Iraq. We remained at the camp for a month. Faisal and Hamzah, like my cousin Ayman Hani, had been indoctrinated into Islam and their radical way of thinking. I didn't know this until we got to the camp. There were hundreds of men at the camp. I became a virtual prisoner of the Islamic State over those four weeks. At first, I was resistant to the ideology. I was literally programmed into their strict ideology. One of the leaders was Dr. Al-Sabbagh. He led the conferences and indoctrination sessions. He selected certain individuals to undergo his naturalization seminars. I was a citizen of the United States and he knew that I was going back; that's why he chose me to be treated with the hypnotic agent, Brevital. It's like truth serum. Once I was given the drug intravenously, I was open to drastic behavior modification; namely, their radical indoctrination."

"Mike, I know you," I said. "This sounds like one of your bull-shit stories. Do you expect me to believe this con? C'mon, you're talking to me."

"No, no," he said, "it's true Frank. It's exactly what happened to me. They brainwashed me to hate all infidels, including you, but I had to keep up a friendly front with you. When I got back to the States, my schooling in Radical Islam continued. Mustafa Salib was the leader of a local cell operating out of the As-Jami Mosque. Salib was intelligent, charismatic, manipulative and brutal. He took me under his wing and schooled me, more than some of the others. As time went on, he learned of my personal relationships. My association with Cindy and you were under great scrutiny. He made sure Anna Zharkov and I were spending lots of time together. I met Anna and sparks flew. We were inseparable. We fell in love."

"Then why did you marry Cindy?" I asked.

"Because she gave birth to my son," Mike said. "No one in the cell except my cousin Ayman knew I married her. Everyone in the cell was forbidden to stray outside our circle. Infidels were to be hated. Mustafa ordered me to prove my loyalty by killing you. Allah knows I tried!" Mike raged. "Our jihad will triumph!"

"How could you Mike?" I lamented. "We were like brothers."

"How could I, how could I?" he ranted "you killed Anna Zharkov. I loved her. After you killed her, I hated you and wanted you dead more than ever!"

"Mike", I shouted, "I thought that you were loyal to this country? You're nothing but a fucking traitor!"

I called for the jailer and left Mike to face the next thirty or so years of his life in federal prison.

Chapter Sixty

Denise was relieved that the whole mess was over. She couldn't come to terms with Mike's betrayal and for that matter, neither could I. That said, we were entering another phase in our life together, marriage. It was Denise's first marriage and my second. Hopefully my second attempt would be successful.

It was an exciting day for both of us. Denise took Metro North into Manhattan to meet me for some lunch and bridal gown shopping. She had a favorite designer and a pretty definite idea about the style dress she wanted.

After lunch at Starbucks, we arrived for our 2:00 p.m. appointment at Klein's Bridals on East 20th Street. It's true that most grooms don't witness the purchase of the bride's dress, but in our case, it was only natural. Denise said there were only two people she wanted to please with her selection, herself and me.

A very elegant woman greeted us. "Hello, I'm Juliette. How can I help you today?"

We introduced ourselves and Juliette showed us to our seats in the lounge. She and Denise perused some photos Denise clipped from magazines and some images on Denise's cell phone. The two women seemed to click. They discussed our budget and timetable.

"I think I know just what you have in mind Denise," Juliette said with a smile.

"I think you do," Denise replied.
They disappeared to the dressing rooms and I sat patiently on a very comfortable white suede sofa. The next thing I knew, Denise returned to

the lounge. She had a beautiful ivory color slim-fit dress, but I could tell it wasn't *The Dress.*

"What do you think Frankie?" she asked.

"It's nice," I replied, "what do you think?"

"I like it," she said, "but I'm not in love."

"I agree," I replied.

After a parade of four gowns in the same, *like not love* category, out came Denise again. She was silent as she stepped up on the bridal platform. I saw her eyes well up with tears.

"This is it," she said. "I'm in love."

"Me too'" I remarked, "Your so beautiful, you compliment the dress."

The dress was a Monique Lhuillier design, her favorite. "It's just what I dreamed of," Denise said, "a silk mermaid style with a sweetheart neckline." Juliette placed a gorgeous floor length veil on the bride-to-be to complete the picture.

Juliette said to Denise, "Are you saying yes to the dress."

Denise sparkled and replied, "I'm saying yes to the dress."

We were one step closer to the altar. We both couldn't wait for the big day.

Chapter Sixty-One

After some of the dust had settled, I decided to pay Cindy Galgano Baraka a social call. We haven't spoken since Mike's arrest. For all I knew she was involved too. Cindy recently moved herself and baby Santino into her late father's home in the affluent suburb of Greenwich, Connecticut. Nick spent most of his time in his Manhattan apartment, but when he needed to escape the frenzy of life in the underworld, he came to Belle Haven in Greenwich for peace and quiet.

I pulled up to Conyers Farm Drive, to a huge Mc-Mansion set on two manicured acres.

A houseman answered the door, "May I help you?"

"Maybe I have the wrong address," I replied. "Does Cindy Galgano Baraka live here?"

"No, you don't have the wrong address," he replied. "Please wait here for a moment while I consult with Ms. Galgano. May I say who is calling?"

"Tell her, it's Detective Frank Santorsola," I said.

"Please wait here for a minute while I find her," he replied.

In a house this size, it could take hours to locate somebody. In a few minutes Lurch returned and walked me through this magnificent Center Hall Colonial to the enclosed patio. Cindy was soaking in the king-sized hot tub. She was really more beautiful without all the make up and big hair she usually favored. A long soft pony tail hung from the top of her head. Black Prada sunglasses framed her soft features.

"Frankie, come in," she said with a large smile. "I'm so glad to see you."

"Thought I'd stop by and check in on you," I replied. I hadn't seen her happy in a while.

"Thank you Dion for showing Frankie in," she said. "Dion, bring me another martini and Frankie, what will you have?"

"I'll have bourbon, neat," I replied.

"Ah, yes I know," she exclaimed. "Dion, bring Frankie a Blanton's, it's his favorite."

I grabbed a chair and said, "So Cindy, I think you made a smart decision by moving into this palace."

"Yes, if you only knew how many times my father begged me to do so," Cindy said. "I was stubborn and I wanted to make it on my own," she said. "I'm a rebel and defied my father by dating Mike."

"As they say," Cindy continued, "I cut off my nose to spite my face. You know my situation with Mike wasn't all peaches and cream. He was a bastard. At first I couldn't get enough of his charm. Then once I got involved with him, it was all downhill. Soon I was pregnant and at a very vulnerable point in my life."

"Is that why you married him?" I asked, "Cause of the baby?"

Our eyes locked. "At that particular time," Cindy said, "that was the choice I made, right or wrong. In hindsight, it was the wrong choice."

A very playful Cindy tried to lighten the mood. "Hey cutie, wanna join me in here?" she asked. "There are some towels right behind you."

"No thanks, I'll take a pass," I replied.

Lurch returned with our drinks and left the bottle of bourbon on the side table.

"That will be all for today, Dion," Cindy said.

"Yes ma'am," Dion replied. "Good day."

"Cindy, I gotta ask you a question," I said. "Were you aware of any of Mike's secret life?"

"Absolutely 100% no," she replied. "He was a cunning guy who never left a clue about that side of him," she said. "Besides, my father wouldn't stand for that shit. I was totally in the dark. Had I known I woulda grabbed Santino and run for the hills of Greenwich a long time ago."

"I bet you would," I remarked.

"I've filed for divorce from Mike," she said. "I want nothing to do with him, ever!"

"Good," I said, "what about Santino?"

Cindy emptied her martini glass in one swallow. "Frank, confidentially, Mike isn't Santino's biological father."

"What the hell did you just say?" I shot back.

"You heard me," she stoically replied. "Santino isn't Mike's son. I have DNA proof," she smirked. "I was seeing a few men at the time. I know who Santino's real father is."

"Do I know him Cindy?" I asked.

"As a matter of fact you do, Frankie."

Now my mind was spinning out of control. Who could it be?

"About two years ago," she said, "I came to visit you in your office. I wanted to talk to you about my father and Mike. Remember?"

"Yes I do," I said. "I vaguely remember. What does that have to do with it?"

"I don't know if you recall or not, but you introduced me to someone that day, someone who would change my life," she said. "He and I were immediately drawn to each other. We began a torrid love affair. We had to sneak around because I knew Mike would kill anybody who wronged him. You know how jealous he was Frankie."

"I would say insanely jealous," I replied.

"You are so right," Cindy said. "I was terrified of him. Anyway my lover and I had fallen deeply in love. We planned to spend our future together. After a while, the constant pressure of hiding our passionate affair from Mike, took its toll on the relationship. We decided to stop seeing each other for a time. I wanted to protect him from the possibility of being killed by Mike. I couldn't live with that. I loved him more than that. I had to protect him, so I ended it."

"Cindy, so the mystery man is Santino's father?" I asked.

"Yes," Cindy said. "I found out I was pregnant, gave birth to Santino and went ahead with the marriage to Mike. Now everything has changed. My man and I are both unattached. Mike will be in jail for twenty years, maybe more."

"Who is Santino's father, Cindy?" I asked curiously. "I have to know."

Cindy rested her head back on the side of the hot tub and said, "Assistant District Attorney Beau Winslow."

Now I've heard everything, I thought to myself. "Does Beau know that he's Santino's father?"

"Yes, he knows," Cindy replied. "He's on top of the world. He said he's never stopped loving me and wants us to be a family. We're planning to get married in a few months after the divorce is finalized. He has always wanted a family."

"How do you think Mike is gonna react to the news?" I asked.

"Well Frank," she said, "as you know my two cousins, Rocky and Gino are involved in my father's mob business. They are gonna deliver the news along with advice that Mike better leave me, Santino and Beau alone."

"Cindy, I'm happy for you," I said. "I hope everything works out for the three of you. I'll congratulate Beau when I see him."

The still rebellious Cindy said, "Frankie, bring me a nice fluffy towel, will ya?" She rose out of the hot tub, wearing only the Prada sunglasses. Her beautiful hot body glistened in the sun. I wrapped the towel around her from behind and gently kissed the top of her head. She had a tramp stamp of a lady dragon.

"Good luck, beautiful lady."

Chapter Sixty-Two

The evening before our wedding the entire bridal party attended the rehearsal at the church. We decided to have an impromptu rehearsal celebration at Jake's Bar & Grill afterwards.

Bobby McCarthy greeted the group, as we arrived. The place was crawling with patrons, we could barely move. Friday night was a night for celebrating the weekend, away from the stresses of 9 to 5 grind. Jake McDonald had hired some live entertainment for the Friday night crowds. The Ginger Trio played some Irish folk tunes as well as some contemporary favorites. In answer to your question, yes all three had red hair.

Denise and I were finally free to be ourselves again without the constant threat of harm that had beleaguered us over the past year. Even Denise's former security detail, Pete Jeffries and John Reilly were here. It felt like old wonderful times.

My groomsmen were all here, Rich, my best man, Ace, Angel and Joe Nulligan. These were the men I knew I could count on for loyalty, friendship and support, my inner circle. Denise and Jessica had become close friends. Jessica was Denise's bridesmaid. Aunt Margret will arrive in New York tonight. She will give Denise away tomorrow.

Tyra and Jorge arrived hand in hand. "Hey guys," Tyra yelled out.

"What will you two have to drink?" I asked.

"Two cabernets, thanks," Jorge said.
Tyra, beaming said, "Jorge and I are getting engaged. We are in love and we don't want to waste any more time."

Denise reached out and hugged Tyra.

"I have a built-in family," Tyra said. "Jorge's two little girls are so adorable. Just like their daddy. I've fallen in love with them too."

"We're going to Disneyworld, next week," Tyra went on to say.

"I'm the luckiest man alive," Jorge said smiling.

"I'll fight you for that one," I said grinning and gave him a wink.

"Congratulations, Frankie and I are thrilled for your happiness." Denise gushed.

Joe and Jessica looked closer than ever. "Joey's physical therapy is really helping him heal," Jessica said. "It's been a tough road for him. He'll be going back to light duty at the office."

"Cheech, I can't wait," Joe said. "I can't wait to get back to work. As soon as I'm fully healed, Jess and I are gonna start planning our future together. We're gonna get out of Garth Road and look for a house in the suburbs."

"Hey guys, that sounds great," I said. "Let's get a house in the same neighborhood." The four of us toasted to that. Just then I spotted Taj Taha at the door. I got his attention and flagged him over. Taj's entry caused quite a stir among the crowd. His date was pop star Mia. She wore her trademark white blonde short wig, styled with heavy straight bangs that covered half her face.

"Hi, this is Mia," Taj said. "What are you doing here Frankie?"

"Denise and I are getting hitched tomorrow," I replied. "We're celebrating."

"You've got quite a bit to celebrate man," Taj said grinning. "In more ways than one."

"I'll drink to that," I replied.

"Speaking of drinks, Mia and I are gonna get ours," Taj said.

Suddenly, Ace spotted his date Coco, entering the bar. He hurried over to greet her. Coco, was a sought after run-way model. Ace proudly pranced her around the room. "Glad you could make it on such short notice," Ace said.

"Me too," Coco replied.

A few of us were gonna grab a bite to eat. We headed for an open booth. What do ya know, seated a few booths away was Beau Winslow and Cindy Galgano. It must have been one of their first public appearances together. They were finally free to flaunt their love. We exchanged hellos and retreated to our booth.

During one of the Trios breaks, Bobby McCarthy stepped up on the small bandstand and toasted us. "Tonight I want to make a toast to a fabulous couple of kids who are taking the big plunge tomorrow," he said. "Whether you know them or you don't, please raise your glasses in tribute to the lovely bride Denise and her very lucky groom to be Frankie."

Bobby finished with an Irish toast. "Bless you and yours, as well as the cottage you live in. May the roof overhead be well thatched and those inside well matched. Slainte!" From your mouth to God's ears, I thought to myself.

The room roared in approval. The clinking of glasses was like music to our ears. Denise and I called it an early night. We had a big day tomorrow.

Chapter Sixty-Three

Corpus Christi Catholic Church in Portchester, New York was built in 1945. My father Frank was one of thirteen siblings. His brothers, Rocco, Lucas "Nuggie" and Tony did much of the stone work and the interior plastering. They were taught the trade from their father Carmine, my grandfather, a master European craftsman. It was a time in the world when great pride and energy was put into your craft.

Fittingly, Denise and I decided to get married at Corpus Christi Church at 5:00 p.m. on New Years Eve. My brother Rich was my best man and my girls, Catie and Francesca were delightful little flower girls. Denise's Aunt Margret walked her down the aisle to my waiting arms, while my daughters sprinkled red rose petals on the center aisle white runner. As I watched Denise gracefully glide down the aisle, I was praying that she and I could maintain the spark of loves beautiful light for many years to come. We tenderly exchanged vows with the promise to love and respect one another till death do us part.

Directly from the church we headed to the New York Botanical Gardens. Aunt Margret gifted us a two hour cocktail and hors d'oeuvres reception. The evening was filled with love. Sofie and her rock star husband, Terrence Plimpton came to the reception. The Plimpton's gifted us with a luxurious two week honeymoon at their Bora Bora home. We four depart on their private jet tomorrow morning.

The honeymoon was more than we could have ever dreamed of. Sofie and Terrence left Bora Bora after a few days to tour Europe with the band. We had the villa all to ourselves and had the time of our lives.

Fast forward fourteen days later; "Hurry or we'll miss our flight home," I said in a rushed voice, "there isn't another one off this island till tomorrow!"

"We'll be on time, don't worry," Denise replied.

The best is yet to come.

Chapter Sixty-Four

Under federal law, acts of terrorism and the penalties for committing these crimes can vary from life in prison, to the penalty of death. This prompted District Attorney Hogan to turn over our entire case to the United States Attorney's Office, Southern District of New York. The case was eventually referred back to AUSA Wilber Jones of the White Plains Office. To keep our fingers on the pulse of the case, Beau Winslow was cross designated as an Assistant Untied States Attorney to assist in the prosecution.

Over the next several months, there was a comprehensive review of the evidence. I'm happy to say that detective Joe Nulligan is back at work and assigned along with FBI Special Agents Desaye and Spencer to conduct the pre-trial investigation. The data obtained from Farid's computer was analyzed and two more operatives of Salib's cell were arrested.

A federal Grand Jury was convened. Imam Mahadi, Ezra Awad, Mike Baraka and the others were indicted for violating Title 18, Chapter 113B of the US Code. A trial date was set for April 15, 2018. AUSA Jones decided not to separate the trials and tried the defendants together.

The defendants were held without bail at the Metropolitan Correctional Center in Manhattan. Mike tried to contact me, but I refused to speak to him. There was nothing more to say. We were done.

It was quite a scene in the courtroom. The defendants were brought in by US Marshals. They were shackled at the ankles, chained at the waist, handcuffed and seated at a long defendant's table. The trial lasted six months. Mike's mother attended the trial faithfully everyday. The defendants were found guilty as charged. Mike was sentenced to 15-years to life for his involvement. Mahadi was sentenced to life in prison without the possibility of parole. The others were held as terrorists and remanded to Guantanamo Bay, Cuba for an indefinite time. We never did find out if sarin gas and explosives planted in an around the city were the work of Mustafa and his cell of fanatics. The fact of the matter is that we never let our guard down and we never will. These ideologues are out to destroy us.

Mike stood in front of the judge as he was being sentenced and as the judge read his sentence into the court record, he passed out. The Marshals revived him and helped him out of the courtroom, as he and the others were led to a holding cell behind the courtroom. They were later moved to the Metropolitan Correctional Center on Park Row in lower Manhattan, awaiting transportation to federal prison.

Interpol located Quan Ly living in Saigon with his new wife Fabienne Do. At the present moment the United States doesn't have an extradition treaty with Vietnam, so for now, Quan will safely avoid American justice. Phuc Nguyen also fled to Saigon and has since opened a restaurant.

DA Hogan promoted me to Detective Captain, replacing C.J. Matthews, who was now the Chief of the department. District Attorney John Xavier Hogan established a new squad, specializing in deep undercover investigations. The new Chief, gave me a free hand in running the squad and in selecting the detectives that I felt had the aptitude for this specialized work. I was married to the love of my life. Man it's great to be alive!

Epilogue

Frank Santorsola (a.k.a) Frank Miranda has spent twenty-seven years in law enforcement and is known for working deep undercover infiltrating organized crime and narcotics investigations for the District Attorney's Office, Westchester County, New York. He ultimately rose to the rank of Chief of Detectives. Frank and his wife, Christina MacKenzie Santorsola co-authored "Honor & Deceit." It is a fictional story and his third in the series of books he has written. They include "Miranda Writes / Honor & Justice," and "The Garbage Murders."

Frank has also been featured in TNT's docudrama, "Family Values the Mob & the Movies," and "The Real Sopranos," by Class Films.

For sales, speaking opportunities for Mr. Santorsola, or other inquiries, please contact us at:

Baxter Productions Inc.
308 Main St
New Rochelle NY 10801
(914) 576-8706
pressoffice@baxterproductionsmedia.com

Photo Credit:

Aleksandr Khakimullin © 123RF.com.
Andrei Seleznev© 123RF.com.

Made in the USA
Columbia, SC
22 April 2019